FIC   Manguel, Alberto.

News from a foreign
country came.

$19.00

DATE			

NEWS

► FROM A ◄

FOREIGN
COUNTRY
CAME

NEWS

► FROM A ◄

FOREIGN
COUNTRY
CAME

ALBERTO MANGUEL

CLARKSON POTTER/PUBLISHERS
NEW YORK

Fic

Copyright © 1991 by Alberto Manguel

Published by Clarkson Potter/Publishers,
201 East 50th Street, New York, New York 10022.
Member of the Crown Publishing Group.

CLARKSON N. POTTER, POTTER and colophon are
trademarks of Clarkson N. Potter, Inc.

Manufactured in the United States of America

Library of Congress Cataloging in Publication Data

Manguel, Alberto.
News from a foreign country came / Alberto Manguel.
p.   cm.
I. Title.
PS3563.A475N48   1991
813'.54—dc20

ISBN 0-517-58343-7

10 9 8 7 6 5 4 3 2 1

FIRST EDITION

R00803 02880

Animula vagula blandula

For Robert Read
gentle, fleeting soul

ACKNOWLEDGEMENTS

T O THOSE who read the manuscript through its several laborious stages, thanks for their friendship beyond the call of duty; to Louise Dennys, my Shahrayer; to Jonathan Warner and Carol Southern, whom I will not call my editors but my readers, and to Lucinda Vardey, not my agent but my friend; to Arthur Gelgoot, without whose generosity, as usual, work would be impossible; to Betty Donaldson and Gena Gorrell for all the hard work on my behalf; to Margaret McClintock for her encouragement; to Sandra and Andrew Goss, in whose house this book was begun; to Maryann Hogbin, of the Ginger Press Bookstore in Owen Sound, for all her kindness; to Richard Outram, for both the conversation and the poem; to Ricki Markwald, who didn't take a question for an answer.

To the Ontario Arts Council and the Canada Council for their support.

News from a foreign country came,
As if my treasure and my wealth lay there:
So much it did my heart inflame,
'Twas wont to call my Soul into mine ear.

THOMAS TRAHERNE

AFTERMATH OF A CONVERSATION

Red blood from the red gills of lumpen fishes
dries on the parched dock. And this is true:
one can imagine having anything one wishes.
Most men don't torture children. But some do.

Admittedly, one can imagine even being wise
in the intolerable ways of man, should he so dare.
The gull, you said, settled to peck out the living eyes
of stranded salmon; my Dear, you do not care

to answer anyone in kind, and not from pride.
To be inhuman sometime fits us like God's glove.
Who may imagine us as creatures who deride
their being God, and being very terrible to love.

RICHARD OUTRAM

HERE

FROM HER WINDOW she could see the beach below, but to reach it seemed impossible, as if the sea and sand and rocks were part of a picture postcard. It was unthinkable to let herself fall down like a bird, like an apple core; instead, she would have to draw back into the house, into the cool darkness of the hall. First she would have to walk past her parents' room; then step lightly to avoid the creaking board on the wooden staircase; next beware the sitting-room where Monsieur Clive would be reading; finally run past the kitchen and Rebecca, the maid.

But maybe she'd be lucky. Maybe Rebecca would be talking to someone and would have closed the kitchen door. Maybe her parents would be out. Maybe Monsieur Clive would be asleep.

Her parents' bedroom seemed empty. She glanced at her mother's large rocking-chair standing with its arms akimbo, and then at a corner of her father's oak dresser. For a moment she felt safe. She tiptoed down the staircase holding on to the cold railing.

"*Bonjour*. Come and kiss me good morning."

Monsieur Clive was standing by the window, looking out into the garden, his back turned towards her. He put his white, freckled hands into his pockets and bent over sideways to kiss her. She breathed in the strong sickening smell of something she did not recognize. She moved her mouth away from his kiss and his lips brushed against her cheek.

"The tree is dying."

She looked out of the window.

"The tree is dying, you see?"

There was a small black tangle of twigs bristling with leaves, erect in the middle of the lawn. Beyond the tree, crossed out by the latticed fence, she could see the bare tip of the beach, and a small white boat on the sea behind it.

"It is called a wild cherry tree. There are no cherries on it now."

Monsieur Clive put his left hand on her bare shoulder. With his index finger he prodded her earlobe. The smell came from his breath.

"Look carefully. You see those clusters of minuscule black seeds caught in the cottonwool web there, in the very hook of the branches?"

As if a spider had spun its nest too quickly, she thought, *stashing away a hundred black flies for lunch.*

"We call them *limaces d'été*, summer vermin. The English call them tent caterpillars. Like worms. Soft, hungry creatures. Long ago they used to paint them crawling out of our bodies, to remind us that they are the true inheritors of the Earth."

She pulled away, but he took her by the hand and held her fast.

"*Viens voir.*"

They went out into the garden.

Monsieur Clive pulled a box of matches out of his coat pocket.

"Watch carefully. *Regarde.*"

He struck a match and, far away, the small boat wavered in the heat. The flame tore the web. The gap widened like an astonished mouth, and four or five tiny black caterpillars dropped out through the charred lips. For a second they held on to the flickering edges, then fell softly to the ground. Monsieur Clive lit a second match. Another hole, larger than the first, spread across the belly of the web. Shreds of grey skin hung limp from the branches, and now handfuls of caterpillars spewed without a sound from the open gash, creatures suddenly blinded by a devouring light, clutching with their whole bodies to wisps of gauze, trying to shield themselves with darkness. A third match exploded in a long flame, blue against the branches, and caught several of the insects in the flame itself. Others began to climb the tree with immense effort, but a fourth flame reached them before they had gone too far. A couple lay writhing by her feet.

Monsieur Clive was no longer holding her hand. He was kneeling by the tree, carefully prodding the corpses with a stick. She walked away towards the lane. He did not call her back.

At the end of the lane was a gate and then, to the right, the Chemin de la Plage. Rebecca was standing outside the gate with Josie Dunkelmeyer. *Rebecca has the shape of one of the girls up at the Indian Reserve*, Mrs. Dunkelmeyer had said to her father in church, *her hair too long, her teeth all yellow*. Mrs. Dunkelmeyer had white, gleaming false teeth that sometimes clicked when she spoke too fast.

Rebecca said in halting French: "He wants to go with you to the beach. And I told you to put on the bathing-suit when you go bathing. A ten-year-old girl should know to put on the bathing-suit when she goes bathing."

Josie was peeling off the leaves from the low maple branches. He ran his hand along the bark, catching the leaves on the way, and then letting the branch spring back naked into the air.

"Stop that. You're hurting the tree."

Josie grabbed hold of another branch. Violently, Rebecca pulled him away, but Josie tore at one more branch and then started racing down the path. With an exasperated sigh, Rebecca slapped a red, ugly hand against her flowered skirt. Her voice mellowed:

"You look after him, for a while, yes?"

No answer.

"I'll bring a piece of cake for you, for the two of you, later. You can eat it under the Rock; that would be nice, no?"

Less out of a wish to obey Rebecca than out of a need to escape the whining voice, she started following Josie down the path.

Rebecca called after her: "I'll be there soon. Be careful."

Then she disappeared.

Now the whole beach lay in front of her, curling around the Rock, announced by a sign that said PLAGE in bright red letters. The brushstroke on the G had dripped. She scratched a drop off with her nail. It looked as if she had cut herself.

From where she stood, she could see Josie run over the rock pools wreathed with seaweed, and across the pebbled strip, and on to where the tide narrowed the path to the Rock twice a day. He looked ridiculously tiny against the huge grey mass of stone.

I don't want to play with him, she thought. She wondered when Matthieu, who was her own age, would be back from camp. With Matthieu she could talk. Sometimes.

A few tourists were out, gathering shells and pottering in the shallow green water. One large man in a white bathing-cap held a pair of binoculars up to where the birds flying in circles seemed as if they were about to be swallowed by an enormous drain. The man lowered the binoculars towards the arch that pierced the Rock and made it famous. "A bridge," her father used to say, "to nowhere." Josie waved and splashed into the water. He appeared to be shouting something at her, but he was too far away for her to understand what he was saying, and besides, the voices of the birds, mingling with the hiss and thud of the waves, drowned almost every other sound.

She sat down on a flat stone and took her shoes off. The image of the dead caterpillars came back to her. She wondered what creatures had once lived inside the shells now powdered to sand, creatures whose skeletons, broken up into countless pieces, quietly slid down her toes. Once, sitting on this same stone, her father had listed for her the three classic impossible things. The first was coining the face of the wind, the second was braiding a rope of sand. She couldn't remember the third one. She scooped up a handful and let it shower down between her fingers. Ribbons of dead bones.

Her mother never came down to the beach. She pictured her on the steep path of pebbles and tangled roots, her mother's enormous weight attempting the descent towards the sea. It never struck her as funny, her mother's heaving size, as it struck others — the neighbours' children, Josie, and the lady from Grande Rivière who came in to do the ironing and who helped Rebecca with her French, in the kitchen, and whom she had seen giggling behind the window as her mother carefully plodded her way across the garden. There was an iron bench in the far corner, painted green, and there her mother would sit sometimes, if the weather was cool but bright, and read a tattered French novel, or knit, soundlessly. Once or twice she had seen Rebecca sitting next to her on the bench, talking in hurried whispers. *As if she were trying not to wake something or someone*, she remembered.

Sometimes her father sat on that bench, smoking his Gitanes, but he preferred rougher weather. In fact, he didn't seem to mind the cold at all, or the heat, and could sit there in the midday August sun, or in the chilly evenings in late May, a big old man looking incongruous in any season, always holding a book of some kind and a pencil in his hands. He wrote on the margins of the books he read, and she had seen in the library whole pages full of neatly drawn letters, underlined words, sentences composed in a careful round longhand which she had once tried to copy, and failed. She thought: *I don't know what my mother's handwriting looks like*.

She wriggled her toes in the warm sand, ten pink animals digging their burrows. Would she grow up to be like her mother? Rebecca had told her that no, never, her bones were all different, and the shape of her face; she was too slim, her cheeks too hollow, her eyes too big, her hair too light, that even before her mother had grown so large she had been a tall woman, a big woman.

In another house, far away, she saw her mother walking like a reflection in a distorting mirror, stretched out from head to feet. Her movements were quick, her voice reminded her of bells. A smell of wax rose from the remembered floor and her mother's arms, strong, not sagging, swooped down to pick her up, while her mother's face, coming forward to kiss her, suddenly broke into pieces like water in the rain.

In spite of Rebecca's denial, once or twice she had imagined herself as her mother was now, vast and round and full of dimples, small eyes sunk deep inside a white face, a small sad mouth that almost never opened, and hair, still black, done up in a rose at the back. She had seen herself like that, and she had tried walking heavily and sitting with overflowing determination in her mother's rocking-chair, moving backwards and forwards, backwards and forwards. One afternoon, as she was rocking silently in the chair, cheeks puffed and hair tied back, she had noticed her mother watching her from the door. She had wanted to explain, *it's not funny, I'm not trying to be funny*, but it had been too late. Her mother had moved away again, out of the frame.

Josie was waving, probably calling her to join him. She didn't bother to answer. A group of women lumbered across the sand, skirts billowing in the wind. Another wave. Thud. Waiting for the next one. Hiss. Thud. Hiss. She couldn't see the man with the white bathing-cap. Someone else, a boy, was holding the binoculars up to the birds. Now Josie disappeared as well. A girl ran by her side kicking sand into her face. The white cap popped up over a crest, then was swallowed again. Maybe the boy would lend her the binoculars. She wanted to see the very tip of the rock, where the birds nested in their hundreds. She'd wait for Josie to come out. He could ask the boy to lend them the binoculars, he wasn't shy.

Under the waves it would be dark. Deep dark, very quiet, words without sound. Long ago, in that faraway house, she had seen an illustration in a children's magazine, flying fish jumping out of the sea into the open beaks of gigantic gulls, a small steamer in the distance, and then, below, filling three-quarters of the page, the green-black depths where lustrous sharks waited for the fish to plunge back in. She saw them blinded by the sheen of evening light, darting back into the water, caught and tugged into the seaweed slime by teeth that in the illustration — the printer had overlapped the colours of the *gravure*, her father had explained — glimmered with a rim of yellow and magenta. Deep, dark, quiet. The title of the picture, her father had told her, was *Terrible Fate of the Flying Fish*.

She saw Josie lift his arms as he raced out of the water, turn sharply and race back in again. *Idiot*, she said angrily. She would have to wait for those binoculars. The man in the white cap had come out and was drying himself with a large red towel.

"Ana!"

She had never liked the sound of her own name.

"Ana!"

Rebecca was coming down the path with a man Ana had

never seen before. Another of Rebecca's friends. Rebecca's breasts bounced as her feet hit the stones on the path.

"Ana!"

"Yes!"

"Where's Josie?"

"In the water."

"It is not too cold?"

Ana shrugged.

"This is Tulio."

The man smiled. One of his front teeth was missing. His skin was darker than Rebecca's. He said something in Spanish which Ana didn't understand. Three years ago, when they had come to Quebec and Ana had started school, she had asked a question in Spanish. The words had hung in the cold air; the class had laughed. The teacher had told her she must only speak French in class. And Ana had promised herself that from then onwards, for the rest of the days of her life, she would never speak Spanish again.

Except numbers.

Numbers were magic.

The man called Tulio tried to shake Ana's hand. His nails were rimmed with black. Ana put out her hand but instead took the cake Rebecca was holding out to her. Sponge cake. With milk jam.

"Go call Josie. I have cake for him too."

Ana lifted herself without uncrossing her legs, then gave a little jump and ran down to the water's edge.

"Josie! Josieee!"

Nothing but the foam on the waves. *White horses, green riders*. No head, no hands.

"Josieee!"

Rebecca and her friend walked up to her.

"Did Josie leave? Did you see him leave?"

The group of women were watching them, holding up their hands to shield their eyes from the wind.

Hiss. Thud.

Rebecca ran towards the Rock. Tulio followed.

"Josieee! Josieee!"

One of the women called to Ana, in French, to ask if anything was the matter.

Ana shook her head.

Tulio kicked off his shoes and plunged into the sea. A huge wave covered him completely, but he managed to lift his head beyond it and keep on swimming. He looked, Ana thought, like a monster in a horror movie, hair stuck to his forehead, shirt stuck to his body.

"Josieee!"

Several other people were standing on the wet sand, looking into the sea. The man in the red towel was there, the group of women, a few children.

Six or seven birds hovered over them and then alighted a few feet away. They waddled around, uninterested.

Rebecca was shouting at Tulio in Spanish. In spite of herself, Ana caught a word or two.

Uno, dos, tres, cuatro, cinco. . . .

A shout over the waves. The crowd parted. Tulio emerged carrying Josie's body, limp, in his arms, struggling through the water. The large man put his towel over Josie, and Rebecca suddenly noticed that she still had in her hand Josie's piece of cake. She threw the sodden mess to the birds.

Squawks.

Mutterings and wailings.

Hiss, thud, hiss.

Rebecca pressed Ana's head against her wet side.

"Oh Ana, Ana. You didn't see? You didn't see?"

Tulio put Josie down on the sand, trying to keep the towel around him. A bit of seaweed was sticking to Josie's right eyebrow. Ana wanted someone to notice it and brush it off. She struggled out of Rebecca's embrace.

"The current. Much too strong," an elderly man was explaining. "For a child. He should have known."

Tulio bent over as if to kiss Josie on the lips. With one hand he pulled Josie's chin backward; with the other he covered Josie's nose. Then he began to blow. Josie's chest rose a little, then sank.

A blond boy whom Ana had not seen before came running up to them.

"I phoned. *L'ambulance arrive.*"

Tulio kept on blowing. The group whispered and shouted. Rebecca held Josie's hand and made small whining noises. The man with the bathing-cap put his hand on Ana's shoulder. The high-pitched siren sounded through the screeching birds, the blond boy pointed to the top of the path, the ambulance men hurried down with their stretcher. One of the women kissed Ana on the cheek and held her against her chest, which smelled of coconut oil. A grey seagull, pecking at something next to Ana, gave a little jump and flew away, and then came back as if nothing had happened. The whole group, skirts and towels and bathing-suits, followed the men carrying Josie on the stretcher, his face wet and white, and in the back, voices kept saying *noyé, noyé, mort noyé*, while the coconut-oil woman led Ana by the hand, trudging through the powdered seashells, past the sign that said CHEMIN DE LA PLAGE, up the path of stones and roots. Through the wind and the voices and the crying and calling of the birds, she picked out the beating of the waves once more, steady as the ticking of a clock, and let herself be pulled away, thud, and hiss, and thud again.

Hiss, thud.

Thud.

Ana ran into her mother's room because she wanted to be enfolded. On the way into the house Monsieur Clive asked her a question, but she didn't even turn her head. She wanted to see her mother's huge white arms open like wings and then close over her, keeping out the light. *Wings of bread*, she thought, remembering the angels made from dough which Rebecca had shown her how to prepare at Christmas. But when she opened the door to her parents' bedroom, her mother was in her rocking-chair, staring quietly at her knitting. Her arms were slowly flapping up and down, creasing at the elbow the wobbly skin, protecting her knitting-nest, to which Ana knew she had no claim. The arms would not open.

"I'll sit here," Ana said, pointing at the embroidered footstool. She waited.

"You know that Josie . . .?"

A nod.

"I want to tell you, I'm sorry."

She felt the words were not right. *You don't say sorry, you say pardon*, her father corrected her sometimes. Pardon for what? The large bird kept flapping, eyes on the clicking needles. One, two. One, two.

"I'm afraid."

Mumble, mumble.

"They took him away. Did you see them take him away?"

Click.

Rebecca sometimes got her to speak. Could she get her to speak?

"Are you afraid?"

Click, click. One, two.

"He drowned."

Drowned, difficult word. Sticks in the throat. *Down, drone, drowned*.

The ancient memory of her mother moving briskly through a room, turning her neck, smiling at her with different eyes, appeared and disappeared.

The large white bird kept clicking its wings.

"Mrs. Dunkelmeyer, when she got out of the car, she was carrying parcels. She had bought things for Josie in Ste-Thérèse."

The bird rose. The arms grew, the sagging flesh fell thinner and thinner till it became a curtain of gauze like the ones which fluttered on the windows in the dining-room. The white round face narrowed, the shrunken eyes sank even deeper, like clam holes in the sand, and with a cry the whole mass shuddered forward. The room became the sea, the wallpaper water. It grew dark, as if great storm clouds had suddenly spilt over the sun, and in its gilded frame a small steamer puffed smoke over the horizon. The great sea-bird plunged into the new cold depths — always fluttering, always clicking away — and for the briefest of glimpses looked down at Ana and said:

"No one ever drowns, no one ever drowns, no one ever drowns."

In her room, Rebecca was crying. Mrs. Dunkelmeyer's face kept rising towards her, like a terrible fish. She, Rebecca, hadn't lost anything, she told herself, *nothing of mine is lost*, but her voice didn't soothe her. Josie lay there as Luisito had lain, in that coffin that looked like a toy.

Five, six years away, in a low whitewashed house in a suburb of Buenos Aires, the neighbours were moving silently, in and out of the darkened rooms, placing a well-meaning hand on her sister's shoulder, her sister, ugly with grief, crouched over the wooden rim of the coffin painted white like a flowerbox in a playhouse.

If I hadn't, if I hadn't, if I hadn't. Her sister kept repeating, over and over, like a litany: "If I hadn't asked Elbio to come back, if I hadn't been so angry at Papa, if I'd sent Luisito away with his uncle, if we had left when El Negro told us." No room to mourn her husband, taken away (the neighbours said) in a black Ford Falcon, bleeding (the neighbours said), calling out for his wife. *Nothing to be done, that's the way things are, bad luck, señora, bad luck.* No (the neighbours said), we didn't see the men's faces, no (the neighbours said), please don't ask us to come forward. What can we say? We didn't see anything, nothing really.

She, Rebecca, had gone back with her sister into the room and she, Rebecca, had tried to stop her sister from seeing Luisito. Her sister's hands had clawed at Rebecca's arms, leaving thin lines of broken skin. And the neighbours: *He tried to stop them from taking his father. Barely eight, a little man. Courage, Señora Eulalia. Courage. What can we say?* Eulalia's hands stopped clawing and lay dead in Rebecca's own.

The neighbours organized the wake, dressed Luisito in his first communion suit, put up the flowers. Her cousin Lorenza came, and Lorenza's husband, and El Negro's younger brother. The policeman who lived a few blocks away came, dragging his wife along, but the neighbours wouldn't let him in. They didn't say anything, do anything. They just stood in the doorway, shoulder to shoulder, and wouldn't move. He asked to be let in, said, "Excuse me," raised his voice. At last he left.

Eulalia wouldn't eat or drink. She wanted to know. "Did they hit my Luisito? Did they push him aside and did he crack his head open on the door frame? They were holding me; I couldn't see — tell me. Did they hit Luisito on purpose? Did they do that?"

"Shh, it's no use asking, Eulalia, it's no use asking."

"But I need to know. I've got to know."

It's no use asking.

Monsieur Clive was standing once again by the wild cherry tree. Nothing seemed to have disturbed it. The bodies of the *limaces d'été* had vanished, gone to earth, ashes to ashes. Purified.

Monsieur Clive was a policeman. His full title was Staff Sergeant Maurice Clive, attached to the Special Investigations Division of the Quebec Sûreté, he always added, but everyone knew him as Monsieur Clive. Not even his superiors called him by his title. He had served in France, in the French army, and in Algeria, and then, as his hair thinned and his subordinates grew younger, Monsieur Clive had felt less adventurous and more nostalgic, and had finally decided, some twenty years ago, to renounce the tri-coloured flag and return home to Quebec. Here, duty had not been a demanding mistress. A special dispensation had allowed him to enter the Sûreté after the age of thirty-five, and a series of quiet cases had followed. "Mainly paperwork," he always said, and meant it as an apology.

He had certainly not regretted being sent on this routine investigation to Percé. His grandmother had used to come to Percé in the days before the little graceless motels and the sordid souvenir shops, in the days when the only place to stay was L'Hôtel de la Plage, now long crumbled back to the sands from where it had sprung. Monsieur Clive had always wanted to holiday in Percé.

Monsieur Clive's fingernails were dirty. He had been scraping at the earth by the garden bench, a little patch that had seemed to him recently dug up, only to discover a grimy bone. A dog's treasure, evidence of a dog's crime. Monsieur Clive fished in his pocket for his Swiss Army knife, unclasped one of the blades, and began to pare the dirt from under his nails. Tiny grey crescents, like shadows of his fingertips, stuck to the knife and then fell to the ground.

Monsieur Clive was careful not to cut his nails in the process. His grandmother had told him many, many years ago that after our death the soul, before it can rest, must collect every one of our nail clippings from wherever we may have dropped them. Monsieur Clive had always been careful to cut his nails over a little enamelled box bought long ago in Djanet.

Monsieur Clive was bored. He had looked forward to spending a few weeks with his friend Antoine Berence, talking about old times, Algiers, the glorious days, the days when the young Monsieur Clive had set out to seek his fortune in the footsteps of Bugeaud and Pélissier. But since Monsieur Clive's arrival in Percé, Berence had deliberately avoided him, made excuses. Not that Monsieur Clive wished to impose. He had called upon his friend out of love, yes, but also out of politeness; he had not suggested staying at Berence's house; it was Berence himself who had offered a room; not too enthusiastically, true, but then Berence had never been one for effusive demonstrations.

Could one lose *l'esprit de combat*? Berence didn't even carry himself like a soldier any more, his sloped shoulders, the half-tired gait. . . . If only he could attract Berence's attention once again, if only Berence would talk to him, from the heart. *Ah, well*, Monsieur Clive thought, *I'm not a great reader, I have no ear for music, I know nothing about painting. He has little to talk to me about now.*

Had married life changed Antoine? Monsieur Clive considered this question. He had met Madame Berence, for the first time, in Quebec City. It had been a shock which he had kindly tried to disguise. Antoine, Antoine Berence, impeccable Antoine Berence, married to this creature?

Antoine had met her, it seemed, in Algeria, not long after Monsieur Clive's departure. Did Antoine talk to *her* about art, about literature?

In the olden days, of course, it had been different. Berence had shown only a private interest in books and concerts. None of this gaudy display of bookshelves. His public interest had been in people. He had watched people with the avidity of a collector, an entomologist keen on discovering why a certain beetle ate only snails, another only rosebuds, a third the obscene flesh of figs. And he wasn't above sharing his discoveries, pointing out to Monsieur Clive quirks of character, idiosyncrasies, mannerisms, human colourings and shapes and sounds. At first Monsieur Clive had thought that here was a man who took his colonialism earnestly. Berence had seemed to want to understand the place in which they were living. He had studied Arabic. He had met some crazy old Frenchman who had decided to become a Muslim, and had spent long nights with him in a smelly little room on Éloise Street. He had played chess with the fishermen. Monsieur Clive had enjoyed his company, and they had become (or so he had always thought) friends, comrades. *Mon camarade* this, *mon camarade* that. That was how they had spoken of one another until Berence had been assigned to Sergeant-Major Grolier, and he, Monsieur Clive, had begun to think earnestly about *La Nouvelle France*, his home and native land. *"Terre de nos aïeux,"* Monsieur Clive hummed thoughtfully.

Monsieur Clive stared out at the Rock covered with birds and bird droppings, and further out at Bonaventure Island. He tried to fix his eyes on one single bird, recognize it, follow it in its elliptical flights, but it proved impossible. His eyes lost the bird, it became another, and another, and yet another. No individuality to it, nameless, faceless, part of a number. Monsieur Clive's knife slipped and cut off the tiniest scraping of nail from his left index finger. Monsieur Clive imagined his soul trying to find that almost invisible nail sliver in the sands below the garden.

Monsieur Antoine Berence was in his room, which also served as the library. He slept with Marianne in the large blue bedroom, where he napped every afternoon from exactly two o'clock to four. But it was here, in the library, that he spent most of his time when he was in Percé.

The walls were almost entirely covered with oak book-cases, with the exception of an inset stereo system which occupied half a wall, and a large bay window at the far end. The window overlooked the sea, Bonaventure Island in the distance, and the Rock, a broken bridge of stone, linked to the mainland when the tide was out.

By the window he had his desk. On the desk were an old leather-edged blotter from Algiers, a wide-nibbed Mont Blanc pen, a ream of white paper with the watermark of a crouched lion, a silver-framed portrait of Berence himself, aged twenty-one, drawn with a quick pencil and signed *Jean Cocteau, 1938*, a blue and white Dubonnet ashtray which his father-in-law had once stolen from a hotel in Marseilles, a packet of filterless Gitanes, a gold lighter bearing an engraved signature which could not be read unless held at a certain angle, a glass paperweight which once (so he had been told) had belonged to Chateaubriand and which the French ambassador in Buenos Aires had given him seven or eight Christmases ago. Most of the objects he loved were here, in Percé, not in his house in Quebec City.

On the shelves were books in English, French, Spanish, and a few in Arabic. You could tell what language they were written in by their condition and colour. The Arabic had cream-coloured and smudged spines; the Spanish and French were tattered and showed the stitches that held the signatures together; the English books had glossy spines with loud lettering, and were larger than the rest. Under-neath the bay window were shelves that held dictionaries and encyclopedias, and a two-volume gazetteer that had belonged to his father, a country doctor in Normandy who had died shortly after Berence's birth and whose face was, in Berence's memory, a confusion of beards and hats and moustaches. There was also a torn photograph, reconstructed and protected by glass, of a crowd in front of a *fin-de-siècle* building, signed *Marianne Berence*.

Framed into the bookshelves was a copy of Dürer's copperplate engraving *Knight, Death and the Devil*. He had owned this engraving since his adolescence, when he had bought it at a Paris flea market, before the war. He had studied it carefully, memorizing the lines drawn by the artist's burin, searching for almost invisible details in the castle on a hill in the background and in the gnarled trees sprouting from the rocks in the Knight's path. He had tried, for memory's sake, to copy each of the figures separately: the Devil, with his stupid spaniel face, pig's ears, and ram's horns, lumbering in the back; Death, old and cadaverous, holding up the sands of time with a grin of *Schadenfreude*; the Knight, the *Ritter*, on his robust and eager stallion, wrapped in armour, hung with weapons, shielded by a warrior's helmet through which the face could be seen, unprotected, clean-shaven, and serene — a creased and thoughtful face which with the years Antoine Berence had come to think of as his own. *Der ewige Ritter*, the eternal horseman, fighting a king's war on foreign ground, risking everyman's death and everyman's damnation. And yet, in Dürer's hands, so singular. One knew he had a name, a home, a past, suffered from toothache, was torn by love, preferred goat cheese to cheese made out of cow's milk, believed in the salvation of his soul, ignored his dog. *Common clay*, he thought, *common dust*. Dürer's engraving dominated the room.

Facing the door as one walked in were two large leather

armchairs, but this was nevertheless a one-man room. The position of the armchairs did not suggest conversation. An interview, perhaps, but no intimacy. A few times Monsieur Clive had come to talk to him here — talk to him, not with him. A cat, an orange cat, a long-haired orange cat with white tufts of fur at the tip of her ears, was lying on one of the armchairs. Clawmarks on the chair's right arm and down its right leg signalled its proprietor. Antoine Berence, smoking a Gitane and balancing a white china ashtray on his knee, sat in the other chair. He was reading a book but wishing it were another. He was trying to remember a few lines from the book he didn't have in order to compare them with the lines he had just read.

Corporal Tremblay from the Percé headquarters had left about fifteen minutes earlier, after telling him, our distinguished Percé citizen, about the drowning of the Dunkelmeyer boy, a terrible tragedy, sir. Monsieur Clive had flashed his badge and Corporal Tremblay wanted to assure Monsieur Berence that he would not be disturbed any further, no need to attend the inquest, sir.

He wondered whether he should go and talk to the Dunkelmeyers. He barely knew them but Ana enjoyed playing with the boy. *Attachments*, he said to himself, *the constant loss*. Down in the village the other distinguished citizens of Percé would be going about their business once again, hardly brushed by the small death at sea. They would have their dinners and discuss politics in the cool of their summer houses, or they would sit around their television sets and wait to be told about the wide and wicked world which never touched their village.

Since moving to Quebec barely three years ago, since their first summer in Percé (he had discovered Percé, "*a razor blade rising from the water*", in André Breton's *Arcane*, read during his adolescence in France under the gnarled rocks of Étretat), he had observed these people much as an ornithologist might observe the myriad of changing seabirds that endlessly circled the coast.

In their eyes, he imagined, he was that mythical figure, the gentleman of leisure come from France, second only to a vacationing film star. These people imposed social obligations on him, neighbourly responsibilities, brushes with hell. But Ana loved the beach. And Marianne seemed happier here than in Quebec City. That above all.

The doctor's little white pills helped Marianne sleep, and Berence had taught himself to love the large slow white form that had once been so strong, so quick. *These things happen sometimes to women who give birth so late in life*, the doctor in Quebec City had said. *A certain depression comes over them, even several years after the child is born. Like the smoky veil that fell over Saint Anne*, he had added, somewhat pedantically, *after the Immaculate Conception.*

Attachments, Berence repeated, with a sigh. He thought again of the lines he was looking for, but he wasn't going to find them today. There was a knock on the door. His daughter, Ana.

He put the open book down carefully, so as not to crack the spine, and knelt down beside her. He took her in his arms, rocked her gently, and said nothing for a moment. Then, finding the position awkward, he kissed her on the lips, creaked to his feet, led her to his armchair, and held her in front of him as he spoke.

"It wasn't your fault."

"But why did it happen?"

"We don't know, my love. We can't know."

"But he won't come back."

"No, he won't come back."

"Does it take long to drown?"

"No."

"But does it hurt?"

"I don't think so."

"Have you ever seen anyone drown?"

There was a slight hesitation.

"Yes."

"Was the person who drowned in pain?"

He had to lie to her now.

"No."

"Does a person who drowns know he is drowning?"

"No one knows. Maybe. Maybe not."

"Will Monsieur Clive be staying long?"

"No."

Ana nodded and asked no more questions.

He wanted to tell her that Josie had done his time, and his time had come to an end. He wanted to tell her that we have all been measured in different ways for different lengths, that we are made of time, like grass or sundials or water. He wanted to make her think of that which has an end we can see, the visible shapes of time, growth and passing and decay, rivers, insects, the clusters of lantana flowers whose stems she liked to suck, the branches on the forest floor covered with lichen, and even the slowly shifting constellations in a darkness that was also dying. It was all so clear, so sensible to him. He had always known exactly the place of everything in this weary world.

But she didn't need to hear that.

So he took her again in his arms, and lifted her to him and held her, and again rocked her very softly for a long time, in silence, as if he, her father, were the immutable centre of the universe, and she, his daughter, a small blue moon circling round him, living off his force and reflecting his light.

Antoine Berence was sitting in the armchair with his daughter on his lap when the cat jumped down from her seat, stretched her hind legs, yawned, and very slowly walked to the door, which had been left ajar, and out into the hallway. Antoine Berence was still there when, almost an hour later, Rebecca knocked on the door to say that Ana's dinner was ready.

Ana ate alone in the kitchen. Rebecca had set out for her a small piece of grilled fish and a tomato salad, and then gone into the garden. Looking through the window, Ana saw her mother sitting on the garden bench and Rebecca walking towards it. She stared back at her plate. She was hungry, and ashamed for being hungry. *I'll only eat half*, she said to herself.

She took the plate with the half-eaten fish and went outside. She could see that Rebecca had squeezed herself onto the bench next to her mother; the bright late-afternoon light framed them in a golden sheen and caused them to throw long shadows on the lawn. Rebecca was talking vigorously. Ana tried to make out what she was saying, but Rebecca's lips were moving too fast, and the sounds were broken by the sea below and the cry of the birds above. She saw Rebecca take her mother's left hand and hold it, and her mother's face turn towards Rebecca with an awkward smile.

She speaks to Rebecca, Ana thought.

In Buenos Aires, she knew, it had been different. Her mother had sung to Ana, and told her stories, and Ana had made up others for her mother in a mingling of Spanish and French. *Uno, dos, tres, cuatro.* Ana had tried hard to listen to her mother's voice in those half-invented memories that rose in her mind before falling asleep, but had failed. She had looked carefully at the only picture she had found of her mother before Ana's birth: a big woman, not a fat woman; a strong woman, with black hair as sleek as polished leather. Her father kept the picture in a drawer in the library, and Ana had found it there one morning hunting for forbidden things. She knew it was her mother, and yet the woman looked so unlike her mother, as if drawn by someone not very clever with the pencil. To Ana, her mother was who she was now; her mother had no past, no youth, no child-hood. Her mother would never die.

Ana stood over the edge of the garden, where the hedge leaned over the cliff, and returned the half-eaten fish to the sea.

Antoine Berence had decided to accept Madame Anneliese Michault's invitation for that same night. And he would not bring Monsieur Clive along.

He would not even ask Monsieur Clive what arrangements he had made for that evening. He wished he had not offered Monsieur Clive a room in his house. But duty called Monsieur Clive to Percé; how could a *camarade* do less than offer him bed and board? *Poor Monsieur Clive*, thought Berence, suddenly moved.

He would go to the dinner, fulfilling his duty as one of Percé's notable summer citizens. And he would take Marianne. Marianne, he had discovered, liked Anneliese Michault.

Once, visiting an asylum in Algiers, he had realized with revulsion that what terrified him was the swelling mass of bodies whose different, individual afflictions had become one, a single mad monster. *If only*, he had said to himself, *one of them came forward with a name, a history, features that would form themselves into a face, adult or child, then, perhaps, I would be able to embrace it.* "They are all God's sheep," the wizened attendant with a mangy red fez had said to him in French. "But He doesn't mind my looking after a few in His name."

It had struck him then, it struck him again now as he was driving down the hill, Marianne strapped in the seatbelt by his side, the utter impossibility of loving a vast sea of humanity. *Love thy neighbour*, yes, the person in whose movements we are reflected, a mirror we polish with coaxing, with example, with lies if necessary, someone properly ordered, well behaved according to our simple rules. But *en masse*?

Marianne, young, long ago, her black hair waving in the dusty wind, her skin so white he had wondered how she could stand in the Algerian sun for more than a few minutes. Now the eyes had sunk into the skin, the hair had been fastened back, even the mouth seemed smaller in a face that had waxed like the moon.

He helped his wife up the steps of the Michault house and rang the bell.

"*Bonsoir, monsieur, madame.*"

A sickly-looking maid opened the door. No announcements, of course. He helped Marianne off with the shawl she had just finished arranging; then unbuttoned his light summer coat. As the maid took their things, Anneliese Michault came towards them, both small hands oustretched.

"Brenda is going to South America next week and wants you to tell her all about it. I've placed her next to you. You've heard her sing? Bill!" — changing quickly into English as a very tall man approached them — "Bill dear, Antoine and Marianne Berence. They have become Québé-cois in what? Three years? Antoine, isn't Marianne looking much better? And Bill, you're in charge of Marianne this evening. You can practise your French. Bill is one of our men in Ottawa, or one of their men, I should say, originally from Texas or somewhere. What is your position exactly, Bill?"

The man called Bill made no attempt to explain. Mari-anne looked up, obediently waiting. *Always that light of panic in her eyes*, Berence thought. He felt wary of leaving her alone, as if she might lose her way among the guests. But Madame Michault had grabbed him by the elbow and was steering him quickly away, towards a thin woman whose profile stood out against a dark gold-edged oil painting.

"Have you or haven't you heard Brenda sing? Brenda, *chère*, this is the man I was telling you about. He knows all you want to know about South America. What was that you sang in Toronto last fall?"

The entrance hall had been flooded with light; now, in the semi-darkness of this other room hung with colossal paintings, the thin white profile turned, and Berence won-dered for an instant whether seen sideways she would cease to have a shape, like a doll cut out of paper. Behind her, in a muddled chiaroscuro, a vast mythological figure was crowning a bad likeness of Samuel de Champlain.

"We are flying to Buenos Aires in the fall, like the geese," said the figure. "Monsieur Berence, you'll have to tell me what to do, what not to do. I've been told not to drink the water."

"Like here," a voice interrupted. "I've been telling people to stay off the water for years."

A man in a Roman collar that seemed too large for his emaciated neck detached himself from a small group beneath the Wreathing of Champlain, nodded and smiled. Berence signalled to a passing waiter.

"A glass of wine?"

He picked two glasses off the tray and handed one to the singer, one to the priest. He took one for himself.

"I'm not saying it justifies this fecundity of spirits, but what is one to do? Do you know that every lake, every river, every patch of water in Quebec is now undrinkable?"

"Père Hébert," said a grey-haired woman bedecked in jewellery, "attributes every geographical disaster to *les orangistes*, eh, *Père*? What was the FLQ going to do about acid rain? And hello, by the way. I'm Félicité Godbout, better known as Madame Lemaire. Newly come to Percé, like the *père* here."

"Certainly not allow it to continue in Quebec, I can guarantee that," the priest carried on. "In the beginning was the Word; that has been taken from us. Then God made earth and water; those were taken from us. You call them God-fearing people, *les orangistes*?"

"I don't mix in politics." The singer gulped down her wine to show her determination.

Berence looked around, suddenly uneasy. He couldn't see Marianne in this half-light.

"You may not mix in politics, but they will certainly mix with you," he heard.

"You are a pessimist, *Père*. I've always thought pessimism should be counted as a mortal sin. Such a bleak outlook on life: blood, proclamations, revolution. . . ."

"*Chère* Madame Lemaire. I don't call that pessimism; I call it vision. Pessimism implies a lack of faith in the mercy of God. I have deep faith in His mercy, tempered of course by His infinite justice."

Then Berence spotted her in a far corner, apparently listening to the man called Bill. Relieved, Berence turned to the priest. "So you believe that mercy should be subservient to justice, *Père*?"

"Certainly, Monsieur . . . ah, Berence. Swiss, is it? Ah, no? French? Normandy, eh, Monsieur Berence? Well, certainly. Our mercy is undermined by impatience. We have no time to wait for His justice. His justice, Monsieur Berence, requires patience. And He has eternity in which to be patient. Wait long enough and every rabbit will fall into His single trap."

"God the Poacher. How bloodthirsty!" The singer pretended to shudder.

"But no, not bloodthirsty. It's a question of balance, you see. You need justice to prevent *le marécage du mal*, the cesspool of evil, from bubbling over. Measure. That's the divine attribute we forget so frequently. Measure."

"An eye for an eye."

"And both eyes for both eyes."

The waiters collected the glasses and disappeared discreetly.

"You mean God prefers us to be blind rather than one-eyed?"

Berence remembered a quote but didn't say it. The unspoken words left a warm taste in his mouth, a happy memory. He glanced again towards the back of the room.

Père Hébert frowned. The frown gave him a comic look. "God is the God of symmetry, remember? *I am who I am.* Symmetry defined through symmetry. And His Son between two thieves, exactly in the middle, one good, one bad."

"Now, now, Père Hébert." Madame Lemaire pointed her fat index finger at him and shook her stiffly coiffed grey hair. "You're just attributing to Our Lord the aesthetics of His painters."

"But of course, madame. Where else would they have learned it from?"

Berence was about to ask about the uses of symmetry in eternity, when Anneliese clapped her hands and in a loud voice commanded them to "pass into the dining-room".

Fate and Madame Michault's seating arrangements separated him from Père Hébert, who, in consideration of his age, was given the head of the table across from their hostess. Candles had been lit, nestled in dark *papier-mâché* flower arrangements, and Berence had to strain his eyes to see beyond his immediate neighbours. Madame Lemaire, sitting next to him, patted his arm in a comforting way. He peered around to find Marianne and caught her eye on the other side of the table. He smiled at her, and he thought she smiled back, and he wished he could reach over and hold her, so that she wouldn't appear so frightened. *As if she were surrounded by horrible shadows.*

Words were coming to him from the far end of the table, submerged, it seemed to Berence, in darkness — Père Hébert's loud voice, Bill asking Marianne something about her travels. He hated the rumble of voices at dinner parties, not being able to hear everything that was said, taking part in shifting scenes of a performance he wasn't able to follow. When his attention returned, the maid was bending down into the candlelight, lifting away the empty avocado shells and replacing them with *sole Montcalm.*

The word "immortality" reached him out of nowhere.

Suddenly Berence felt he wanted desperately to leave. He wanted to stand up, rise into the surrounding darkness, lift Marianne by the arms, and disappear through Madame Michault's doors. He did not want to follow the conversation, be courteous to these people, offer them his time, his thoughts. *Drift away through an ink-black sea*, he thought, and looked down into his plate.

Between the hostess and the man called Bill sat a tall man with white hair and a bushy white moustache. He mopped up some of the sauce with a piece of bread and began to speak, just as a drop dribbled down the corner of his mouth. The candlelight caught his glistening tongue as it darted out to halt the drop of sauce, and failed, and he was forced to lift the napkin up to his drooling chin.

Everyone waited.

"It's. . . . It's certainly the most popular of literary subjects," he said apologetically.

"Immortality, professor?" Madame Michault repeated politely.

With his mouth full, the professor mumbled: "Sirebmmrtl. Excuse me. I meant the desire to be immortal. The desire that this party never end, that pleasure never reach its culmination." And, helping himself to white Bordeaux: "That the wine in this bottle last throughout eternity!"

"That's assuming life to be pleasant and happy and fruitful," said the man called Bill. "There are places where life is a nightmare. Imagine, a never-ending nightmare."

The hostess had a *frisson*. She carefully put down her knife and fork, and reached for one of the pineapple-shaped salt shakers.

The professor had gulped down his fish and now felt more at ease to talk. "First the obvious ones, of course. Faust, the Wandering Jew, Dracula, Tithonus, King Arthur locked away in a tree. Ulysses, who wants to remain young through wandering. Then those with hidden motives: Penelope and her weaving, Scheherazade making a short story long. Sleeping Beauty, of course. . . ."

Madame Lemaire nodded. "Our *père* was just telling us that the reason behind eternity is to allow God's justice to prevail. Are you saying, my dear professor, that we poor mortals are wishing for more time just so we can pay old debts?"

"I couldn't say why, I couldn't even guess why. I'm not a poet, thank God. I'm a professor. I just point out a few literary facts."

Berence observed Père Hébert leaning towards Marianne and whispering something in her ear. Her cheeks shone with an oily glint. Would she talk back to him? Once her voice had been breathless, full of fire, it had taken possession, spread out in circles, stopping at nothing, eager. Now it lay still, and Berence wanted to coax it out of its hiding-place, lure it back.

"*Ô Dieu, qu'est-ce que donc que la voix?*"

The maid withdrew the fish-plates and set the salad bowl in front of Madame Michault.

"And why would you ask for a reprieve, Monsieur Berence?" said the singer.

He took a moment to think. He saw Marianne alone, Ana alone with Marianne. He saw them walking through rooms he didn't know, days without hours. A reprieve? He shook his head.

"I wouldn't," he said.

"But surely you wouldn't refuse immortality, if it were offered to you, would you?" Madame Michault asked, piling green salad onto her plate, which, in the dim candlelight, looked like a heap of refuse.

"Yes, I think I would," he said.

"Pardon me," the man called Bill butted in. He pointed at Berence with his fork, eclipsing one of the candles. "Pardon me for asking, but what do you do for a living, Monsieur Berence?"

"I'm retired."

Madame Michault wanted to show off. "Antoine is being modest. He may be retired now, but he was once a very important man in France, *n'est-ce pas, mon cher?* And widely travelled — North Africa, Latin America. . . ."

"In politics?"

"In the army."

"We, monsieur, don't have an army to speak of," Père Hébert called out from his end of the table.

"That is because we are peaceful people. The Switzerland of the North," interjected Madame Lemaire, helping herself to the salad.

"A land of secret poor and idle rich," Père Hébert shouted. "A modern description of Hell!"

Madame Michault laughed politely.

Berence, who had refused the salad, took his eyes off Marianne. It occurred to him, *if suddenly the responsibility for the universe itself were to land on the shoulders of these pretentious people, if suddenly their chatter were to acquire profound importance, would they continue like this, unaware or uncaring of their intellectual misery?* But now he was here, among these ghosts. He might as well take part in their conversation.

"Solomon in all his glory," quoted the professor.

Berence turned towards the little priest. "*Père*, I would have thought you of all people approved of a class system, of an order. The hierarchy of Heaven reflected on earth, no?"

"Order, yes, Monsieur Berence. But what we call order is merely convenience. I approve of the order in the all-seeing eye of God, an order of which I myself am ignorant. In the end, the choice is His, you know."

"*The eye was in the tomb, and stared back at Cain,*" the professor insisted.

The candles had shrunk and seemed to draw in the darkness.

"*Père*," Berence said, as if he and the little priest were the only people in the gloomy room, "in this order of God, I would not want to be chosen."

"You want death to wipe your slate clean."

"I long for tidiness, *Père*. For things to be in their place, the way they should be, the way I want them. But I myself, Antoine Berence, I certainly don't need to be there to see it. My own death is of absolutely no importance."

"You want the party to go on without the host," said the priest, in the flickering light.

"Oh, that would not be very kind to me, my dear Antoine," said Madame Michault, reaching across to slap Berence on the hand.

Once again the maid appeared, *deux ex machina*, and served strawberries and sabayon.

Père Hébert had been thinking. "I don't believe God would do that, Monsieur Berence. Sparrows in His hand, you know. Anonymous as birds under the gaze of our dying Lord. He can't just let you go, a piece of clay that didn't turn out right. This is one of the things that move me most about our horrible world. That if one of us went missing, not dead, of course, but removed, vanished, any one of us, the sorriest, the world would fall like a tower of matchsticks. You are as essential to the world as the sun, Monsieur Berence. He can't just forget you. On you hangs the universe."

Across the table, Berence could dimly see Marianne trying with fierce concentration to spear a strawberry. And the question returned: *When did the fall begin? At what point did she escape, become large as a lake, diffuse, far from me? As if time had stopped for her, covered her stones with moss and lichen, circled her with bushes of thorns.*

He felt he no longer wanted to carry on talking. He smiled across the darkened room at Père Hébert, then at his hostess. He suddenly felt enormously tired. Once again he wanted to go home. With relief, even gratitude, he heard Madame Michault suggest they all move into the living-room. He stood up, helped the soprano with her chair, and as surreptitiously as possible glanced at his watch.

Eleven-thirty.

In the room next to Ana's, Monsieur Clive was trying to sleep. He felt betrayed by Berence's escape, and sorry for himself. He felt foolish for feeling sorry, and angry for feeling foolish. Small acts of unkindness such as this reminded him that he could no longer hope to be a success at what he did. There had been little glory in the French Army days, one more soldier among so many soldiers; there certainly was no glory in the Quebec police force. He was too old, too dull. Behind his back, he knew, his colleagues wondered why he hadn't retired. To what, he wanted to ask them. To walk around the house in threadbare slippers, to long every night for the evening news because it might, just might, bring a spark of excitement? He had seen his brother — wife dead, children away somewhere west — drift into an anonymous old age, unwashed, unattended, sitting in front of a flickering TV set, eating stewed fruit out of a tin. The memory of a vanished voice — his grandmother's, perhaps? — called Monsieur Clive to order. He turned the cool side of the pillow up against his cheek. Tomorrow he would speak with Berence. Now he would sleep.

But sleep wouldn't come. Work spread itself in front of his closed eyes, arranging and rearranging itself. Folders, memos, boxes labelled with the names of the cases he should be working on, well-meant schedules hardly ever kept. "Special circumstances, final test," the lieutenant at the Sûreté headquarters had said, his breath full of cloves. "Last chance." Monsieur Clive's eyes ran down the list of *Things to Do*, ticking off the items.

He tried, once again, to lose himself in darkness. He imagined a black, limitless space and entered it. He saw that he saw nothing. He relaxed his muscles: arms, legs, neck. He observed himself closing his eyes in the dark.

An edge of red light started to break through the borders of his vision. His mind refused to give up, grind to a halt. The light became brighter. He could see dust and white buildings and a hot shimmering sky. Men in long striped kaftans swept along yellow streets. He and Berence were sitting at a table, minuscule cups of coffee in front of them. A group of Arab men were standing at the corner, smoking and talking in loud voices. From one of the narrow alleyways came two European girls in school uniforms, grey dresses, blue hooded capes, white socks, black shoes. The girls walked hand in hand, looking straight ahead. They couldn't be more than seven, maybe eight. From a balcony someone shouted a few words. The men laughed, pushed one another, then started throwing cigarette butts at the girls. One of the butts landed exactly inside the hood of the taller girl. The hood started smoking. The girls screamed, the men laughed louder. The coils of smoke rose delicately into the air. Monsieur Clive couldn't tell whether the smoke he saw came from the rim of the hood or the rim of his cup of coffee. He looked towards Berence, immobile at the table, as if the scene were taking place on a rickety stage and Berence were the sole unamused audience. To Monsieur Clive his friend had seemed as dignified as a cypress tree, as unshakeable as a mountain.

As Monsieur Clive leaned over to peer more closely into the circular, fuming darkness, the light behind his eyes died out and he allowed himself to fall, softly and silently, into sleep.

As Ana opened the door, she realized she had walked into the wrong classroom. The teacher, Madame Frechette, was not at her desk. Instead, a man with a dark face grinned a toothless grin at her, and pointed to one of the benches in the front row. None of her old classmates was there. The other seats were occupied by students she had never seen before, older students who looked eighteen, twenty. Adults. She turned around and saw a lady with curly blonde hair huddled into one of the seats at the back, next to a tall skinny man in a brown suit and a spotted tie. Ana wanted to say that she had made a mistake and leave, but the man at the teacher's desk put a finger to his lips, pouted and shook his head. Out of the corner of her right eye she saw — she thought she saw — Josie, running down the school corridor in his swimming trunks. She looked at the blackboard.

Someone had drawn there, in blue and green chalk, round faces with dots for eyes, doodles like the ones she had made on the Jules Verne book her father had given her for Christmas. He had noticed the doodles and flown into a rage, angrier than she had ever seen him. He hadn't hit her — he never hit her — but he had made her very frightened.

She noticed that the people around her were whispering (*Why are they whispering?* she thought) and then the woman behind her began to sob. Ana turned towards her. The woman had taken off her hair as if it had been a wig, and sat there, bald and wrinkled, tears streaming down her cheeks, making her mascara run. The whole face seemed to blur in tears, as if they came from Ana's own eyes (*Why am I crying?* Ana asked herself). The woman stopped suddenly, pulled a large handkerchief from her pocket, and placed it over her hairless head with ugly red hands.

Ana opened her eyes. The room was in complete darkness. The voices, still muffled but now angry, rose towards her again. She turned on the light above her bed. The faces of her dolls stared back at her. Rebecca's voice, then the voice of a man, then another man, filtered down from the ceiling.

She got out of bed and peered out into the hall. Both the door to her parents' bedroom and the door to the room of Monsieur Clive were closed; no light shone from underneath them. Only the small round window over the stairwell rose in a shimmering blue circle, divided into four like a fairy pie. Ana climbed the stairs to the attic.

She knew she should knock, but she didn't. She simply pushed open the door to Rebecca's room. The sloping roof made it look like a room in a doll's house. Rebecca's bed, probably meant for a child, fitted exactly between two walls and a tiny window the size of a serving dish. The only other piece of furniture was a round red metal table on which Rebecca had placed a mirror, a box decorated with seashells, and a white plastic picture frame with several photographs. There were no chairs. Rebecca and Tulio were sitting on the bed. Another man, with a short curly black beard but no moustache, was sitting on the floor, his back against the wall. He stared up at Ana.

Rebecca jumped to her feet.

"Ana! What are you doing here?"

"I woke up. I heard voices."

Rebecca lashed out something at the man on the floor, who shrugged his shoulders and answered back. Then he stood up and turned to Ana, smiling.

"She is a good girl. She will not tell anything."

Rebecca put a hand on Ana's shoulder.

"Ana, these are my friends. Juan. And Tulio you know."

Ana stood with her hands behind her back. The floor felt cold under her bare feet.

"Ana, your parents. . . . They wouldn't like it if they knew I brought my friends here. All right? You won't say nothing?"

"But why are they here?"

"We come talk to Rebecca," said the man called Juan, suddenly revealing a gap between his teeth. "We are friends, we come talk."

Tulio stood up and started to speak to Rebecca, very quickly. *Uno, dos, tres, cuatro. . . .*

Rebecca seemed angry. She answered in a loud whisper, pointing at Ana, then at the men. Tulio nodded and turned to Ana.

"What you do if someone asks?"

"Asks what?"

"About us, Rebecca's friends, coming to her room."

"Leave her alone," Rebecca said.

"I want to know. Let her answer."

Suddenly Ana was afraid. She clutched Rebecca's hand.

"Leave her alone, I tell you."

"Ana?" Tulio insisted.

"I don't know."

"You'll say no, okay?"

The man called Juan tugged at Tulio's sleeve. Tulio ignored him and waited for Ana to answer.

"Yes. I'll say no."

"Good girl." Tulio patted her on the head.

Rebecca took Ana by the hand.

"Time to sleep now, yes? I'll take you."

Then she turned to the men, said something in Spanish, and, stepping into the hallway, closed the door behind her.

In her own room, in her own bed, Ana felt sleepy again. She caught Rebecca's hand.

"Stay a while."

"I have to go, Ana."

"Just a while."

"Well, just a while."

A beam of light, like that of a lighthouse, streamed through the curtains and drew a white gash across the ceiling and over the faces of Ana's dolls, sitting on their shelf in the corner.

"What was it like, Rebecca?"

"Buenos Aires?"

"Yes, Buenos Aires."

Ana pronounced the name with a French drawl that Rebecca always found funny. She had sat with Señora Berence teaching her the correct mouthing of the sounds. *"Bu-e-nos Ai-res, Bu-e-nos Ai-res."* Señora Berence had laughed and given up. She often laughed then.

"You know, Ana. You remember."

"Rebecca, tell me."

"Very different."

"Very different how?"

Rebecca smiled, as if a little ashamed.

"Different."

Ana snuggled against Rebecca's large chafed hand, which reeked of lemon-scented detergent.

In the evenings, Rebecca began, in the summer, they used to sit outside, because the streets were different there, with trees growing out of the sidewalk. They sat on low chairs, their backs against a long white wall of chalk, the kettle and the twin aluminum container for sugar and *mate* placed carefully on the sidewalk tiles. "There was Papá, and Tía Anita, and the boys, Jorge and Luis, and sometimes my cousin Lorenza, who worked for your mama before I came, and my sister Eulalia, the one who was a teacher. And her husband Elbio, and my nephew Luisito. But that was before."

Names, names, names, names. She saw the street and the wall again, and the smell of a certain Sunday rose to her nostrils. *Tuco*, the thin spicy tomato sauce. Papá moved his small wicker chair under the shade, Tía Anita took off her right sandal and scratched her left ankle with her big right toe, the boys switched on the soccer game on the radio, and Eulalia got up and went in saying she had a headache, but the truth was that she hadn't heard from Elbio in over a week. They all stirred again, once more. And where had she been sitting?

"Go on, Rebecca. Don't stop."

"What can I tell you? Why do you want to know? You were so little when you lived there, just a baby. Go to sleep."

"Tell me. What did you eat?"

"Every Sunday we had *ravioles*. Tía Anita would start early, very early, beating the pasta, you know, like this, and then stretching it over the kitchen table till it was thin like paper. My sister Eulalia prepared the *tuco*."

She had wanted a big party for her fifteenth birthday, but Papá said they'd have to see, what with Jorge out of work and Luis going to Salta, and that good-for-nothing Elbio leaving Eulalia here with the kid. Eulalia heard him. She had just picked up Luisito from his siesta, holding him, a bundle of wet clothes ("that boy, eight years old and still pees his bed"), on her way to the bathroom. She started to scream at Papá, the boy clinging to her like a monkey cub, how dare he, how dare he. Papá looked down and put his hands over his ears, but Eulalia kept on screaming, didn't he see, Elbio was doing this for us, for all of us, you bastard, didn't he see, Elbio didn't want to end up a useless old man like Papá, a dishrag, a damn ass-licker who never dared ask for what was his. Where was his pension, where was his sick pay, what happened to the money the company had promised to set aside for him? Eulalia wanted to know that. And Elbio might not be here, but she, Eulalia, was working, working her ass off, if he wanted to know, because no one, not even her own father, was going to keep her. Nine hours at that rotten cashier job and anything else she could find besides that. But what was he, what was Papá doing? Taking a long time to die, that's what, taking up room, taking up money. Then she ran with Luisito into the bathroom and slammed the door. The frosted glass pane shattered. Sobbing, Eulalia called out to her to get the broom and dustpan.

"Will you make *ravioles* for us, Rebecca?"

"Your father don't like pasta."

"Will you, for me, please?"

"Maybe. Now go to sleep."

Elbio came back one night soon after that. She heard Eulalia get up (she slept with Luisito in the room next to Rebecca's), cross the patio, and go to the door. She heard them make love that night, the creaking bed hitting against the wall in spite of the towels Eulalia put on the brass knobs to muffle the sound, Eulalia's stifled cries, Elbio calling out her name, *Eulalia, Eulalia*, over and over again, as if he had freed it, a bird in a hall of mirrors, after not saying it out loud for so many days. Somewhere in the distance she could hear the bass strumming of a radio.

A car screeched in front of the house. Doors slammed. Poundings, cracked wood, broken glass. Rebecca got out of bed. Papá shuffled across the patio in his slippers, tying his dressing-gown. Before he managed to reach the door to the street, four men burst in, faces covered, machine guns in their hands. They pushed Papá against a wall and ran into each of the rooms around the patio. Eulalia opened her door and started screaming. Rebecca slammed hers shut. Scuffles, shouts, then silence.

Rebecca opened her door again. On the floor of the patio was Eulalia. Jorge, unbelievably asleep throughout the assault, was standing by the broken furniture, asking questions. Papá was bent over Eulalia, heaving, swallowing great gulps of air. *A fish*, thought Rebecca, *on dry land*. In Rebecca's room a lightbulb, covered with a small pink handkerchief, was swinging over the rumpled bed. The rosy light shone over Luisito's body in a corner, then swung away. When it swung back again, she saw blood on his face. Then darkness. The third time the bulb swung over him, she didn't look. She helped Papá get Eulalia on her feet, walked her across the patio to the kitchen, and shouted at Jorge to go down to the Mendietas' and phone the hospital. Through the splintered front door, neighbours in pyjamas and nightdresses began to cluster in small curious groups, asking questions. When the hospital doctor came into the kitchen to tell them that Luisito was dead, Rebecca was waiting for the coffee to drip through the brown cloth filter. Eulalia began making noises like a small hurt animal, and

Papá let himself fall sobbing into his chair. Doña Mendieta took the dripping coffee out of Rebecca's hands and sat her down between her father and her sister. Only when she saw that Doña Mendieta was pouring out the hot dark liquid, the tropical smell rising to her nostrils, did she begin to cry.

Ana dressed as quietly as possible. Through the drawn curtains she could see a bright haze spreading slowly over the water and the sand, picking out glints of silver in the Rock, and smudges of yellow, red, orange, scratched onto an overcast sky. Soundlessly she closed the front door and walked, once again, down the Chemin de la Plage. She thought of Josie.

Somewhere behind the hills was the cemetery, where Monsieur Clive's *limaces d'été* would find their way to other trees, from branches to roots, from roots to earth, from earth to the coffin where Josie lay. Given the choice, she'd have preferred the sea, even if she feared the unthinkable depths and its blind grey sharks, the darkness and the deaf silence. She screwed her eyes shut and put her hands tightly over her ears. Brilliant kaleidoscope shapes swirled around in front of her, geometrical patterns wrought of gold and silver. Rooms in a palace. Who would she play with now that Josie was gone? She stood once again at the foot of the Rock.

A sprinkling of fishing boats was bobbing up and down on the choppy sea. The birds began their racket, swirling over her head and on to Bonaventure Island. Could she count the swarm, more like insects than gulls, dotted high above? *Uno, dos, tres, cuatro*. She missed Josie. She didn't want him to be dead. A large grey gull waddled up to her and pecked at something not more than a foot away from where she stood, cocking its head to the side. Slowly she bent down and picked up a stone, turned it in her hand, and then flung it with all her strength at the bird. The stone caught it on the back. She heard it squawk and then saw it open its wings and fly away across the beach. She watched it for a long time. It seemed to her that it lost its balance once or twice as it soared forwards and back towards the water. And then it disappeared. Had it fallen? Ana felt her eyes fill with tears. She felt suddenly very ashamed and unhappy and alone. She turned to climb up once more and saw a small figure standing at the top of the Chemin de la Plage, shielding its eyes from the growing glare. Monsieur Clive.

"Gathering the roses?" he asked when he reached her halfway down the path.

She didn't know what to say to that. Monsieur Clive stretched out his freckled hand, but she ignored it. "I was only out for a walk," she said, and then, "Everyone else was asleep."

"Everyone except yours truly." Monsieur Clive brushed off the sand from his trouser cuffs. "I've always been an early riser." He seemed to hesitate. "I'm sorry about your little friend."

For a second, Ana was overcome by a confused feeling of both pity and revulsion — gratitude for the sorrow and something akin to nausea at the thought of this birdlike creature being touched by Josie's death. She lifted her eyes to look at him. His smile broke the spell.

"And how long now till school begins?"

"September."

"You must be looking forward to that, eh? Seeing your

comrades again, telling them about your adventures by the ocean. . . ." He stopped by the gate. "Tell me, you and Rebecca, are you good friends?"

"She's a grown-up."

"Yes, I know. But sometimes children and grown-ups become friends, no? You like to hear her talk?"

"Yes. She tells me things. About Buenos Aires."

"And does she tell you about herself? If she likes Percé?"

"I think she does. She has friends here."

"Ah, yes. Friends. What kind of friends?"

"I don't know. Just friends."

"And what does she talk about with her friends?"

"I don't know. They talk in Spanish."

"Spanish. There's a language I've always wanted to speak. *Viva España.* But you know, I'm not good at languages. I suppose I'm lucky to have been born in a French-speaking country. Because if I had to learn it. . . . Hopeless, utterly hopeless. Have you heard me speak English?" Monsieur Clive let out a little laugh, and said in a declamatory tone: "My tailor is rich. Your tailor is poor."

Ana pushed the gate open and ran towards the house.

The clock on Antoine Berence's night-table read 7:30. Beside him, Marianne was heaving, moaning softly in her sleep. He tried to sit up, but a sharp pain shot up his lower back. He tried to relax, but the pain burst again, knotting itself around his sphincter. He closed his eyes and tried to visualize the site of the pain. He said to himself that if he could see it, if he could actually give the pain a shape, he would be able to soothe it away, to coax it down. A swelling.

A growth of sorts. With a gentle finger he reached down his backside to his anus. The pain clotted itself into a rubbery knob, smaller than he had thought it to be, protruding from within, the snout of a reptile. He forced himself out of bed and dressed carefully. After breakfast he would visit the doctor.

Pain changes all, he said to himself. *Mantegna's* Dead Christ, *the yellow skin your skin, the open wounds your wounds, the same foul breath from the still mouth.* He winced as he walked out of the room. *The pain here, now, inside. Maybe there is no other way: eliminate the spectator, be within. This is what it's all about, then. Not pleasure, but pain.*

He was having coffee in the dining-room — standing up; he could not bear the humiliation of a cushion — and staring at a small item in the back pages of *Le Devoir*, a crippled child beaten to death somewhere in the Eastern Townships. He was about to fold the paper over when Monsieur Clive walked in.

"Antoine, Antoine, Antoine."

"Good morning. Have you had coffee?"

"With the birds. You know me. Can't sleep after six. And *I* wasn't up till all hours last night."

"At your age, you need rest."

"Antoine, Antoine. We both need rest."

"If you say so."

"Antoine, you could have warned me."

"Warned you?"

"That you were going out to dinner."

"Don't be absurd."

"I need to know what's going on. I can't fight you as well. If I'm to get somewhere in all this, I need your help. You know the people of Percé, Antoine. I don't. Comrades in arms, Antoine. Antoine, you promised that if I ever needed anything. . . ."

There was something so ridiculous about Monsieur Clive's pleading that Berence forgot his discomfort for a moment. He felt he had to be generous.

"I will, from now on, tell you everything I do. Let's begin this very moment. At 8:30 precisely I'm going to the doctor's."

The kitchen doors swung open and Rebecca came in to lay out Marianne's breakfast. Berence put down his cup, gave Monsieur Clive a military salute, and left.

The tiny waiting-room at the surgery was empty.

Are there categories of pain? Berence thought, not for the first time. *I mean, is the pain felt by a hunchbacked child thrown against the metal bars of his crib different from that which, say, Stevenson felt, lungs grated away by coughing spells, the eyes turned inwards towards the secret open sores spewing blood? Or my own — the pain of one who can see both, understand what the child can't begin to conceive, possess what Stevenson so arduously coined? What category of pain is this, then, a rat turning inside me, growing, bloated? And why?*

An image began to form, a half-memory. A room of white tiles. A single lightbulb. Figures moving in silence. The sound of water. All vaguely reminiscent of a monastery. *Where am I?* Berence winced. He flooded the image with black ink — a second too late.

The door opened and the nurse told him that the doctor would see him now.

All morning Ana tried to be alone, and all morning people swarmed around her like birds. Monsieur Clive, and the man from the hardware store, and red-eyed Rebecca fussing over breakfast. And as she walked past the Chemin de la Plage, Juan in his curly black beard smiled at her. She forced herself to smile back, walked on, but he joined her stride with laborious concentration, as if she were a small animal of some sort, too brisk, too unpredictable. The road ended at the foot of a small church no longer in use. The windows had been boarded up, with the exception of a small porthole-like opening, gaping shreds of blue and red stained glass over the peaked door. Exactly half the church gleamed white in the sunlight, and half stood in the shadows. Ana sat down on the darkened side and pulled her knees up. Juan lowered himself beside her.

"I'm sorry about last night. We frightened you. We didn't mean to frighten you."

She nodded.

"That man, Clive, spoke to you. He asked you questions?"

More nods.

"About Rebecca?"

Something was moving the clump of yellow grass just in front of her. She peered at it but saw nothing. She imagined herself small enough to hide inside that clump. Insect world.

"Ana, I will tell you something about Rebecca."

Wings tucked in under a hard burnt-chestnut shell, legs quivering, a beetle prodded its way onto a patch of red dirt.

"Something happened to Rebecca a long time ago."

"Something like what?"

"And for that reason we must be very kind to her."

"What happened?"

"Her family was killed."

"All her family?"

"Almost all."

"Where did it happen?"

"In Argentina."

"I was there."

"Yes, I know."

"She doesn't seem sad."

"One — how do you say? — recovers."

"Like with Josie."

"Yes."

"I see."

"Ana. You must not tell people about Rebecca. I tell you because you like her. You like her, yes?"

"Yes."

"Some people do not like her."

The beetle climbed onto a small clump of dirt and stopped there, its antennae shivering. Then it scuttled into the shadows and was gone.

"I don't think Monsieur Clive likes Rebecca."

"No, I do not think he does, Ana."

Juan rose to his feet, waved at her, and walked off towards the town.

"Madame Lemaire."

"Monsieur Berence. How nice. I'm replacing Dr. Petras — he's in Quebec City."

Berence felt terribly uncomfortable. He had known Petras for several years, had discussed with him the aches and discomforts of old age, had heard about the doctor's plans to open a clinic somewhere along the coast, had invited him to dinner at the Gargantua and compared the North African seafood to the creatures caught in this cold North Atlantic. Now he'd have to become suddenly intimate with a large, grey-haired woman.

"Thoughts of immortality troubling you in your sleep?"

Berence smiled politely.

"Not at all. Something much baser. Hemorrhoids."

"Ah, the bane of a civilized old age. Let's see."

As he undressed, as he undid his belt and lowered his trousers and his boxer shorts, as he looked upon his white thighs speckled with sand-coloured spots, as he tried to remember those same thighs brown in the sun, the sense that someone was watching him from an inconceivable future suddenly struck him like a blow. It seemed that this old woman, this bereaved Norn, sat singly in a time that was to him unreachable, an inexorable and tangible present that however had not yet taken place for him; that he, delayed in a slower, meticulous past, was still young, still inexperienced, still eagerly curious about the last pages in the book, while she, she and the rest of the world, were waiting for him to catch up with his aged self at a point where all had been resolved and no questions were asked any longer. He wanted to think that, like Mantegna's Christ, this body was the mystery, but that another, the invisible, beautiful self of the past, was even more mysterious because it could not be spoken of. *Mustes*. Close-mouthed, bright-eyed seeress with her hand over her lips.

He climbed onto the steel bed, onto the thin mattress covered with a starched white sheet, and, following Madame Lemaire's instructions, rolled over onto his right side, curled up like a neolithic mummy. The prodding began.

"I'll try to be gentle. A beauty, I'm afraid. This is the source of great reflections, don't you agree? Pain in the hidden parts of ourselves. I wonder sometimes if what Eve hid from the Lord was not her backside. The knowledge of excreted evil. Awful swelling. It must hurt like hell."

He heard her ungloving her proctoscopic hand. In front of him, on the wall, several framed diplomas certified Dr. Félicité Godbout's abilities.

"I'm Madame Lemaire, in my husband's honour, at parties, but for all serious events I'm Dr. Godbout, in case you were wondering. My *nom de plume*, if you like. Don't move. We'll have to deal with that in a draconian manner. Unless you care to leave it to chance. I'm all for the knife."

He nodded, and felt sick in his stomach.

"This will hurt only a little."

He hadn't seen her fill the syringe and now the disinfectant opened a cool circle on his swelling. Then the needle entered. It seemed to plunge in, sharp as ice, and continue down his leg, drilling through his muscles, down to his feet. A cramp seized the arch of his right foot. He writhed.

"Keep still, please. Now, once more."

Again and again the needle bore down on him, but each time the pain weakened. In the end, numbness set in. Whatever Madame Lemaire was doing, it was in a blurred realm of touch, half felt in sleep. Suddenly it was over.

"Well, that's it. All gone. You go home now and sleep."

He turned around carefully. On a stainless steel tray were several scissor-like instruments and pieces of gauze soaked in blood.

Madame Lemaire, Dr. Godbout, was smiling.

"You won't be able to scare him away, you know," Matthieu answered.

It was Saturday, and they were sitting on the wooden railing outside the video arcade. Like mechanical birds, the machines were humming and chirping behind them.

"Scare who?"

Sometimes she envied Matthieu, one of the few friends who actually lived in Percé all year round.

"Him." Matthieu made it sound obvious. "Josie."

"Josie's dead."

"That's what I mean. They come back. Drowned souls."

Ana didn't want even to think about it. She started to walk away.

"Wait. Look, I'll show you."

Towards the eastern end of the town, the road split in two. One branch continued to run along the coast, high above the beaches and the small weekend cottages; the other worked its way into the hills and then joined the main highway south. About a mile down this second road was the old cemetery. Ana had seen it several times, when her father drove past it on his way to Ste-Thérèse or sometimes when he took what he called "the fancy way" into Quebec City. A church had stood next to it once but had burned down many winters ago. The stony foundations were still visible, like the shell of a large cracked egg, edges charred and broken. The tombs themselves, enclosed by a single chain fence, were marked by whitewashed stones. Most of the names on the stones had been erased.

It took them almost half an hour to reach the cemetery. Matthieu pointed at one of the tombs.

"That one."

Ana stepped across the chain fence. The earth looked as if it had been turned over recently, and the grass, still attached to it, lay yellowing in the sun.

"That's where they buried Jean-Luc Gignac, two summers ago. The boat overturned and he was gone. When they found him at the dock of Bonaventure, his face had been pecked by the gulls. They brought him here because his parents had been buried here, and they had to get special permission. There was a procession and the children from Sacré Coeur carried crosses made out of flowers and Père Hébert spoke the words over the tomb. But then," Matthieu lowered his voice, "when someone visited the cemetery a few days later, the tomb had been dug up and the body had disappeared. Madame Holman said afterwards that she had seen the face of Gignac outside her window. And my mother swears she heard Gignac speak to her early one morning, in the kitchen."

Ana looked again at the dug-up earth, and then, far away, at the gulls swarming back and forth over Bonaventure Island.

"No," she said.

"My mother says those who drown don't die. They become shadows. Real shadows. Shadows you can see."

"Josie's dead."

"Josie's drowned."

"What your mother says is nonsense."

Suddenly, Matthieu jumped over the chain fence and turned to face Ana.

"My mother's right. You don't belong here. You and your crazy mother and your father with his nose stuck in the air. You think you know more than all of us. You don't know anything."

Ana tried very hard to keep the tears out of her eyes.

They walked back in silence.

As they entered the town, a gannet, the ochre stain on its head gleaming in the last rays of the sun, swooped down and sat itself on a railing. It flapped its black-tipped wings once, twice, and then remained stone still except for its head, which turned to follow them as they passed, staring with blue-rimmed round eyes, while the dark feathers of its forehead seemed to melt and run like ink in thin streaks down to the end of its beak.

As Ana opened the door, Rebecca was at the kitchen table slicing fish. From behind, her long black hair swayed to the movement of her arm, and Ana, forgetting Matthieu, stood still for a moment, mesmerized.

"Close the door. You let the bugs in."

Ana sat on the long bench by the side of the table. Rebecca picked up the white meat and tossed it in flour and herbs. The moisture soaked through.

"Rebecca."

"Yes."

"You didn't tell me your family had died."

Rebecca had chopped onions, garlic, and chives, and now she scattered them over the oil glistening in the pan.

They sizzled as they fell. She wiped her hands on a teacloth and stirred with a wooden spoon.

"Was it when I lived in Buenos Aires too?"

The ancient smell of frying onions filled the kitchen. Rebecca dropped the tossed fish into the pan. She stirred once again, and sat down.

"Who told you that?"

"Your friend, the one with the curly beard."

"He should not have told you."

"How did they die?"

"They were killed."

"All of them?"

"My nephew. Both my brothers. My sister-in-law. My brother-in-law. My father."

"And your mother?"

"No. She died when I was little. A long time ago."

"How old are you, Rebecca?"

"Twenty-one."

The wooden spoon fell to the floor with a clatter. Ana picked it up and handed it to Rebecca. Rebecca wiped it on the teacloth.

"Who killed them?"

"The police."

"Why?"

"In my country, the police don't need reasons."

"And I was there?"

"You were living there. Yes."

"Was that why my parents brought you here?"

"Yes."

"Do you like my mother?"

"Yes. Very much."

"Because you knew her when she was different?"

"I liked her very much then. And I like her very much now. Your mother is very good. Very kind. And very clever, too. Even if she don't speak."

Rebecca dipped the spoon in the pan and tasted the cooking with the tip of her tongue. The smell filled Ana's nostrils.

"Rebecca. . . ."

"What?"

"Did anyone in your family ever drown?"

"Yes."

"Who?"

"My brother Jorge."

"How did he drown?"

Ana waited.

"He was drowned."

"You mean by someone?"

"Yes."

"Who?"

"One of the men who worked for the police."

"Why did he do it?"

"Why did he drown Jorge? Because Jorge would not tell him something he wanted to know. So he held his head in a bucket of water."

Rebecca put a lid on the pan and sat down. She spread a newspaper in front of her. From a basket on the table she took a large, grey potato and started peeling it. As the potato peelings dropped in spirals onto the paper, Rebecca's fingers changed colour, mirroring the dirt.

"Rebecca."

"Yes?"

"Does Jorge come back sometimes? Do you see him?"

The potatoes, now small dirty corpses on the newsprint,

multiplied at an extraordinary speed. They whirled in Rebecca's fingers, carved by the sharp knife, swept in a small wild dance that stripped them to the flesh.

"Sometimes. When I remember."

"No, but really. Does he come back? Is it true that people who are drowned don't die?"

Rebecca stood up, gathered the potatoes in her arms and went to wash them at the sink. As she was putting them on to boil, she said:

"Don't believe all that nonsense, child. The dead are dead, drowned or not."

And then she added:

"It is those who do the drowning who have no rest."

When Ana turned her head to look out of the window, the sun had gone down and a huge grey moon hung in the sky.

Propped against pillows in the master bedroom, Berence was listening, as he did every Saturday, to *Ein deutsches Requiem* by Johannes Brahms. Marianne was silently moving around the room, rearranging bits of furniture, straightening out books and ornaments, dusting the invisible dust off every surface she saw. She was like a large and blind beast gently going through the motions of a routine whose significance had been forgotten, actions that in all probability had no reason any longer to be. She moved gracefully, her full form floating through the space between objects, paradoxically, with the ease of something ethereal.

Slowly the orchestra led to the first, soft words, sung haltingly: *Blessed are those who carry a suffering. Selig.*

Soulful. *Leid*. Suffering, pain. Then, conviction built. Individual voices seemed to buttress the rising chorus. The bass, remote at first, came forward, underscored by the strings. The ghost of a happy theme passed through and vanished. The chorus found solid ground. Suddenly something happened, something that did not *need* to happen in the music — an irruption, a creation. Sounds became coloured by this new knowledge. Ah, the beauty, the beauty of it! If he could only see, like Brahms, that far, then nothing would surprise him, he thought. Chrysalis. Cocoon. The architecture of the thing! Everything already that which it will become.

Berence was no longer suffering. The swelling had disappeared and the discomfort of bowel movements had eased off. The painkillers made him drowsy, but after a week of them he knew how to use the drowsiness to his advantage. At last he could, he thought, master his daydreams.

Now the whole orchestra prepared itself for the next movement. Firmly, grasping the space created by its sounds, it preached in a deep, determined voice its overwhelming truth. The chorus sang out that all flesh is grass, and all beauty like the flowers in the grass. Grass that is wilted, flowers that will die. *Such tenderness in the horror*, Berence thought, not for the first time, *such meekness*. Ah, the beauty, the beauty! Who had said that Brahms wrote "as if God had approved of it"?

From under half-shut eyes, in a pink mist, he saw Marianne, her head turned towards him. He felt like an underwater swimmer watched from a distance by a large, silvery fish. She came near him. Her plump hands patted the pillows, pulled the light eiderdown up to his bristling chin. He had let himself go, he would shave tomorrow. He would

have a shower — not the hot salt baths Madame Lemaire
had ordered — and shave and put on a white shirt. He'd
sit out in the garden, in the sun. He smiled gratefully at
Marianne. As soon as she saw his smile, she pulled away.

A feeling of immediate recognition came over Berence.
He watched her move knowing exactly how she would move,
like someone rereading an interrupted page in a familiar
book.

Another woman had moved like this, the neck turned
upwards, the eyes on him, in a darkened room, to another
music.

Berence had been young, an officer in his late twenties,
accompanying Madame Georges Bidault, wife of the French
foreign minister, on her official business of guiding Important Female Personages through Paris. In the hall of the
Hotel Meurice they had been kept waiting, and Madame
Bidault, with a swirl of her summer furs, had just ordered
Berence to see whether the Personage was indeed coming,
when the grilled doors of the lift swept apart like theatre
curtains and the Personage stepped out in a black dress
splattered with blood-red roses. She was astounding.

Berence had heard Perón compared to Mussolini: he had
expected him to have a fierce and dowdy wife. Evita was
like a doll cut out of a fashion magazine.

That night, at the Alcázar, Evita sat in a cloth of gold
spread out as large as the table itself, Monsieur and Madame
Bidault to her left, the Argentine ambassador to her right.
She spoke, over the moaning of the *chanteuse*, in a French
that reminded Berence of vaudeville Spanish, of her convoys
of gifts sent to the poor across her country.

To Madame Bidault, she said: "The high-class bitches
in Argentina didn't want to make me head of their charity.

They said I was too young. I told them, fine, if they couldn't accept me, they should name my mother."

Madame Bidault laughed politely.

The *chanteuse* left the stage and the master of ceremonies announced a comic act. Two clowns appeared dressed as a camel, doing a tap dance to the tinkle of a piano. Evita clapped. The dance ended and the camel backed towards the official table, producing from its rear a bouquet of flowers which it offered to the guest of honour.

Evita stood up, drawing with her both the ambassador and the foreign minister.

"I think I now have a clearer understanding of French culture," she said in Spanish.

The ambassador translated.

Then: "You must be proud of your achievements," she added, with a curtsy.

And she turned her neck exactly as Marianne was turning hers now. He watched her with admiration, with respect.

He had thought then that he could love a woman like that.

Marianne was moving towards the door.

The music came back to him.

The theme had grown. Meekness had turned to strength, the wrath of the lamb. Time shall pass, but not triumph, because everything passes. The immortality of memory, the drop that wears down the mountain. Time is a delusion.

The orchestra called up the drums, the room rang full of warning. The future had been abolished.

Then, suddenly, silence.

"Surely this loud music is not right for the sickroom."

Monsieur Clive had stopped the tape recorder. Berence

lifted himself a little higher on the pillows. Marianne left the room.

"Clive, you are too accustomed to giving orders."

"How are we feeling?"

"We were feeling splendid until a few seconds ago."

"I'm sorry."

Monsieur Clive looked around the room.

"Marianne certainly keeps you comfortable. She looks . . . calmer somehow than in Quebec City. More peaceful, yes? The country air, I suppose."

Berence made no answer.

Monsieur Clive continued.

"Antoine, listen to me. There are things I must do. One of them is speak out."

Monsieur Clive sat down on the bed. With distaste, Berence noticed that Monsieur Clive's tie — rust red — had an oily stain in the very middle. He tried not to look at it.

"Antoine, we must talk."

No, we mustn't, Berence thought. *We must draw curtains to muffle unpleasant voices. Live in the present. There is nothing I can do for you, old Clive, faithful Clive.* Aloud he said:

"Not now. Please. I'm tired."

Monsieur Clive's shrill voice persisted.

"I wouldn't ask if I didn't need your help. But this is a difficult assignment, Antoine, and I must succeed. And you know the area, you know the people. You see the unusual. You've had experience. When I told you I was being sent to Percé, you asked me, you insisted I stay with you. And I thought, my assignment concerns Latin American poli-

tics — Antoine will help me. How fortunate that I know
Antoine, that I'm his friend."

Berence closed his eyes, darkening the room against the
intrusion. *I won't recall the past, not even for friendship's
sake. Dear Clive, I can't help you. Your knowledgeable
Antoine is sunk in an ink-black sea; I threw him away to
find some rest. Your bloody business is your own. I've cut
away. I remember nothing. Leave me in peace.*

He must have said the last few words out loud because
Monsieur Clive's voice seemed absurdly close to tears.

"Antoine, if you don't want me here, I can stay at the
auberge."

"Of course you're welcome here. We will talk. In a few
days."

Monsieur Clive took Berence's thin, long right hand in
his, squeezed it, and stood up. Before leaving, he switched
the tape recorder on again. Now with full conviction, the
chorus insisted once more that all flesh is grass.

On Tuesday, her day off, Rebecca suggested to Ana a picnic
on Bonaventure. "But ask your mother," she added.

Marianne was sitting on the garden bench, doing — so
it seemed to Ana — nothing. When Ana asked her about
the picnic, Marianne nodded and smiled, and then did
something unusual. She stretched out her arm, plump and
dimpled, and reached for Ana's hand. Ana let her take it,
and for a moment mother and daughter remained motionless, one sitting, one standing.

"Be careful," Marianne said, mouthing the words.

The voice startled Ana and she took a moment to answer.

"I will, *Maman*." Then she leaned over and hugged her.

As the small boat bobbed up and down towards Bonaventure, Ana followed the flight of the birds circling above them. *Among them*, she thought, *are the ones that pecked out Gignac's eyes*.

The boat drew a wide circle around the island and then docked on the northern side. Signs guided tourists to the appropriate roads, but Rebecca ignored them and walked off along the path that rimmed Bonaventure Island to the east. They reached one of the abandoned fishermen's huts set away in the high grass, and stopped to look inside. The timber was worn and grey, and half the ceiling had collapsed in the back room, which had probably served as sleeping-quarters. When they emerged, Juan was standing outside.

"Isn't this good?" Rebecca asked her. "Juan decided to come too. ¿*Qué suerte, eh?*"

"I don't believe you," Ana said fiercely.

"What do you mean?"

"You knew he'd be here. That's why you wanted to come."

Rebecca turned to Juan and said something quickly in Spanish.

"All right. There in the back. We'll sit down and talk."

A tree had fallen a few feet away from the house and lichen had covered it with very fine embroidery. They sat by it, Juan hunched on his heels.

"Ana. I told you about Rebecca. Remember?"

"Yes."

"It is the same with us."

"What do you mean?"

"We all have lost family in Argentina. I and Tulio. And many others you did not meet."

"Is that why you are together?"

"Yes."

"But why don't you want anyone to know?"

"Because the friends of those who killed our family would want to stop us."

"Here?"

"Yes."

Rebecca said something in Spanish; Juan answered. Then, to Ana:

"Rebecca told you that one man drowned her brother. Yes?"

"Yes."

"That man was responsible for many things. Things done to Tulio's brother. And to friends of mine. And to me."

Rebecca held out her hand, as if to stop Juan from moving. Angrily, he spoke back to her in Spanish. Then he rolled up the sleeve of his blue shirt. As he kept folding the cuff over itself, Ana saw, snaking up his arm, a zigzag line, purple and welted. She knew it was not a vein; the segments were too perfect, broken fastidiously at equal angles.

"We want to find the man."

Juan rolled down his sleeve.

"You understand now. Yes?"

Ana nodded.

She noticed that a long line of ants was marching up one of the branches of the tree, carefully following the baroque convolutions of the lichen, dangerously close to the handle of the picnic hamper by Rebecca's side.

"If we find him, Tulio and Rebecca and I will see that he is punished. Then we will go away. And still you must not say anything."

"Will Rebecca leave then?"

"Yes."

Ana turned towards Rebecca:

"I'll miss you."

"I'll miss you too. Are you still angry?"

"No."

"Then let's have lunch."

Rebecca reached sideways, put the hamper in front of her, and opened the lid.

"Ana. Is it all right if Juan joins us?"

"Yes."

Not a single ant had crossed onto the hamper.

Antoine Berence tapped with his fork on the knife Monsieur Clive was holding:

"Your hand. You have not yet learned the North American manner. You continue to be a Gallic barbarian, ready to pounce upon whatever is on your plate as if it were something to kill. You hold the knife in one hand, the fork in the other, waiting to attack. Learn from the land you live in. Here, in the New World, while your right hand pecks gently at the food, your left hand, in true Christian fashion, lies resting in your lap, oblivious of the world. Once it has served its purpose, it abandons its weapon and retires from strife. Watch, my dear Clive, and learn. There's a lesson."

"You mean I too should retire, give up?"

"No one can judge that but yourself."

"You don't believe what I've been telling you."

Between them, on the white tablecloth of the Gargantua, sat an elongated saucer full of tiny pink periwinkles, *les bigorneaux*, each one ringed with perfect violet lines, like fingerprints. Leaning on the rim of the saucer were two glistening pins. Berence put down his fork, pushed aside the half-eaten *quenelle* on his plate, took one of the pins in his right hand, a *bigorneau* in his left, and began pulling the animal from its delicate-looking shell. He shifted in his chair, still a little uncomfortable from the operation.

"You tell me that a group of Argentinians has arrived in Quebec looking for a man. You believe that the man they're looking for is in Percé. You believe that Rebecca, whom we brought here from Buenos Aires, is involved in their activities. You believe that they will do something to someone soon. Am I correct?"

"Yes."

Quickly, with a twist of the pin, he ripped out the minuscule body and put it in his mouth. *Would we eat them if we knew they felt pain?* he asked himself, distractedly. *Miserere nobis.*

"Clive, Clive," dabbing at the corner of his mouth with his napkin. "Is the Sûreté really so inefficient, so badly informed? I lived in Argentina, Clive. The military were a bunch of bungling ignorants, but so were the guerrillas. High-school recruits, Clive, fighting against peasants with high-class ideals. Little armies of boy scouts against uniformed village idiots. These were not the FLN, these were not the OAS. Your 'quarry' is safe, Clive. These *guerrilleros* can kill, yes, but it's more likely they'll blow off their own heads than pull off a complicated vengeance. And certainly not your garden-variety Rebeccas. You can tell our man Bill not to worry."

"Bill?"

"Isn't he the one you were thinking of? Madame Michault expounded on his 'Argentinian experience'."

"Perhaps. We don't know."

The waitress took away the *bigorneaux* and *quenelle* dishes and laid down a huge platter of crab legs between them.

"Not green but the colour of sunset," Berence quoted from memory. Doré's illustration for the seventh circle of Dante's Hell — the murderers turned into a dusky wood, *"gnarled and matted thick, and thorns instead of fruit, with poison filled*", the suicides running among them, pursued by black dogs. Would these crab branches bleed if he broke them? *"From the broken splinter burst both words and blood."* He cracked one open. Would these bones speak? A long, tender pink thorn appeared from its casemate.

Monsieur Clive wasn't eating.

"Bill reminds me of Lenoir, remember him? Thin but all muscle, got a liver infection from a tattoo needle. Yes?"

"I've ordered his file."

"Clive, you've grown old, old, old. The only mood left in your conversation is the imperative. And you hardly eat any more."

Berence picked up several crab legs and piled them on Monsieur Clive's plate.

"Clive, Clive! In Algiers there was hardly a night when the tables were not cleared before we finished talking. Where is the Clive I knew then? Once you explained to me the passing of time, you told me you believed there was no present. We only see what has been, the light of stars long dead; we never catch up with today, you said. And then you said, when we die, we'll never know it is happening. You were a philosopher, Clive."

Monsieur Clive tore off a piece of bread and put it in his mouth. He glanced at the dead crab legs.

"Are you making fun of me?"

"Fun?"

"Haven't you changed too?"

Berence poured Monsieur Clive some more wine. *Dear eloquent blood.* "Not changed, Clive. I've settled."

"You say that as if to exclude me."

"Clive, you're welcome to stay at my house for as long as you like. But I'm retired. Let each of us stick to the decisions he has made. You have been asked to hunt. I have chosen to read, listen to music, drink wine with my friends. I have read my life away, as someone once said. I wouldn't ask you to sit at home with a book."

With a small smile that wrinkled the corners of his eyes and mouth, Berence lifted his own glass to his lips.

"Fine." Clive smiled back. "To each his own. I won't bother you again. I'll carry on with my chase, and you can bury yourself in your study."

And Monsieur Clive stood up, picked up his plate of untouched crab legs in his thin, freckled hands, and threw them across the table into Berence's lap.

Several guests turned in surprise to watch a quarrel between two elderly gentleman.

"I won't take anything of yours then, Antoine. Forget the time we shared. Forget the friendship we had. I trusted you. I was proud of our past. But you are like a blind old walrus, making your nest comfortable and crushing everything in your way!"

Suddenly Monsieur Clive realized that he was shouting and that the manager of the restaurant was hurrying towards them.

He sat down.

"I'm sorry," he said. "Please forgive me. Perhaps I had too much wine."

Berence cleared the food from his lap, being careful not to drip the liquid within the crab legs on his trousers, and reached over to pat Monsieur Clive on the arm.

"It's all right," he said to the manager.

And then, to Monsieur Clive, "We are friends. Of course we are friends. Throughout eternity. Those who do violence to others, such as policemen, and those who do violence to themselves, men who bury themselves alive in books, like myself, both share the same circle of Hell, did you know that? You will be made into a knotted tree, groaning and spewing blood, and I'll be chased by black female mastiffs over your aching roots. We'll be together, my friend."

The manager of the Gargantua cleared his throat, took a seat, and, pulling out a pencil and a notebook to add up their bill, asked them in a thick Normandy accent, as if nothing had happened, how they had enjoyed their meal.

The next few days it rained. Ana kept to her room, playing alone. The adults seemed quieter somehow, more hushed, and Ana woke up every morning to a peaceful sensation of silence and warmth, and fell asleep every night to the sound of the rain.

One morning, very early, she had gone downstairs to watch the rain from the dining-room windows, and had seen her father standing in his pyjamas, looking out at the sea.

He had called her to him, and they had stood together for a while, watching the grey colours become tinged with light, opening in torn gaps to the sky behind.

"Rebecca's mother," Ana said, "told her that God has three keys: the key to life, the key to death, and the key to the rain."

"If you believe in God," said Berence.

"Do you?" Ana asked.

"Once, somebody I knew became so much inflamed with the idea of God that it consumed him. It burned him up, completely, until there was nothing left of him but ashes."

"You saw it happen?"

"I saw the ashes. Others who knew him said that the miracle was a proof of his holiness. But I don't believe it was. You don't need to prove the existence of a God to fall in love with God. If this landscape outside were a dream, would you love it less?"

Ana considered this for a moment.

"Maybe," she said. "If I knew it was a dream."

A week before the beginning of school and the tiring ride back to Quebec City, Ana asked Rebecca to teach her the Lord's Prayer in Spanish. By Sunday, Ana had memorized it and was ready to repeat it in church.

Berence decided that they would walk to St. Anne's. He had expected his wound to have healed by now, and yet at times a pull or twinge would remind him of its presence. He told himself that rest was not helping. He should exercise. He fetched Marianne's shawl, put his raincoat over his shoulders, and took Ana by the hand. Marianne held on to Rebecca's arm and slowly, absurdly dignified, they moved up the road towards the small church.

Here we are, Berence thought, *to please the parishioners*, *one of the paradigmatic images of civilization. The Family, on Its Way to Church.* "Art pompier." *Put a gilded frame around us.*

As they sat down in their pew, Ana noticed Mrs. Dunkelmeyer a few rows behind them. Mrs. Dunkelmeyer tilted her head slightly to one side and smiled. Ana looked down.

She can't have forgotten, can she? Ana asked herself. *How dare she smile?*

If she looked back, high above the entrance, she could see a large painting of Saint Anne, the mother, leading the Virgin child to the Temple. *Dedicating her child to God,* her teacher had told them. *Returning the immaculately conceived child to her Maker. At every birth,* her teacher had said, *Saint Anne stands guard.* Her patron saint, guardian of beginnings.

As Père Kennin stood up to read the homily, Berence noticed that Père Hébert was standing at the altar. He nudged Marianne and nodded. She looked at him and followed his gesture, and looked back at him, enquiringly.

"Père Hébert, remember?"

She shook her head.

Père Kennin began his text.

"Matthew 18, verses 21 and 22. This is the word of the Lord. 'Then came Peter to him, and said, Lord, how oft shall my brother sin against me, and I forgive him till seven times? Jesus saith unto him, I say not unto thee, Until seven times: but, Until seventy times seven.' This is the word of the Lord. Amen."

The congregation responded.

Père Kennin continued.

"Seventy times seven. Four hundred and ninety times are we to forgive our brother, our sister, our neighbour, the man who lifts a finger against us, the woman who speaks evil about us. Four hundred and ninety times, says Christ Our Lord. But what of the four-hundredth-and-ninety-first time? What of the time when the required amount of forgiveness has been reached? When it seems that we are no longer told by Christ himself to forgive the sin against us? What then?"

Père Kennin made a long pause.

"Are we allowed then to effect our revenge? Are we allowed then to lack compassion?"

Another pause.

"As we deal with others will the Lord deal with us. For every grain of sand that we put in the balance, He will cast a boulder on the platter. For every fly He will demand a son or a daughter. For every time we close the door against our neighbour He will raise a forest of fire and a cleave a river of ice. Because" — and here Père Kennin's voice lowered almost to a whisper — "it is He, not we, who alone holds revenge in His hands. Let us pray."

The chorus prepared itself for the hymn, one or two members coughed, the organ sounded its first notes.

After lunch, Berence went to the library, and sat down with the orange cat on his lap. Even though he felt drowsy, he would not go and have his nap before two o'clock. He enjoyed the notion of keeping a routine. Mrs. Dunkelmeyer, who had slowly waddled over to greet them, shaking hands with Berence, kissing Marianne on both cheeks, had told them that she had seen Rebecca leave a few minutes before the end of mass. Berence, politely, had asked Mrs. Dunkelmeyer to visit them — "maybe, maybe, but I'd hate to impose" — and then Marianne had put her hand on his left arm, Ana had held his right, and once again the Berence family had become a living tableau for all to admire.

Now, in his room, Berence felt too sleepy to read, too lazy to put on a record. His *Ritter*, frozen in a stride between the Devil and Death, caught his eye for a long moment. *When I die*, he thought, *this is the image I want to see*. He felt his eyelids grow heavier and heavier. Finally he put the cat down on the floor and climbed up to the bedroom.

Marianne was lying on the bed, eyes closed. She had taken off only her shoes. Her large stockinged feet rested like two furless animals on the blue eiderdown. Her chest was heaving, and her mouth, slightly open, made small distressed noises. She had let her hair out of its net and it lay loose over the pillow.

He lay next to her. He remembered how he had loved — so many years ago — the curve of her neck, the slight dimple behind her ear, the richness of her hair. He turned on his side, towards her.

He put his arm around her chest, and let his fingers climb the far side of her face, reaching her earlobe. Marianne frowned in her sleep. He propped himself up on an elbow and bent over to kiss her, very softly.

She opened her eyes.

Her dress was made out of pale blue cotton and it was done up in the front with a long row of buttons. He began to undo them, starting at the top. When he reached the bottom one, the pale blue cloth fell limp to both sides of her body.

He reached underneath her, between the dress and the skin of her back, to unclasp the bra. Trying hard not to hurt her, he managed to force his hand under her and reach the clasp. It gave way. He lifted the bra off and her breasts fell to either side.

On his knees, he crawled down to her feet and, one by one, pulled off her stockings. He noticed the long veins marbling her thighs. He reached up for her panties and tugged at the elastic waist. By the time he had taken them off, he was out of breath. He felt a small pain under his ribs. He paused.

He remembered her then, but Marianne now was — he thought — even more beautiful. Age had softened her lines, sagging the muscles of her arms, creasing the skin around her waist, covering her legs with dark spots like dull constellations. Her hair was still black, except for a few white brush-strokes at the temples, but the face it framed had bloated and paled like something left too long in water. *Weathered*, he thought. And kissed her again.

She made a small noise and turned her head. But her body remained on its back, the dress like an open cape caught only around her arms and shoulders.

He got off the bed and undressed, watching her. Then he climbed back once more, next to her, running his hand over her with great care, so that only the very surface of his fingers touched her skin. Up, down, across, his hand traced her forms, and he remembered more. At last, very quietly, trying to control the wheezing in his lungs, he lifted himself over her, entering her as gently as possible, burying his face in her hair, rocking up and down, trying not to weigh too heavily on her, till he could hold himself back no longer.

When Berence looked up again, his wife's eyes were still watching him, but she said nothing. She lay there, he thought, as if the lovemaking had happened to someone else, in a faraway kingdom, a long time ago.

If the number of boards along the floor is an even number, Ana said to herself, *Rebecca will come back. I'll get up tomorrow morning and she'll be there, making breakfast in the kitchen, smelling of detergent. I'll call down to her and she'll answer, and I'll ask her to make sponge cake with milk jam. But,* Ana said to herself, *if the number is uneven, then I'll never see her again. She'll be gone as Juan said she would, or she'll have died in a horrible accident. She'll be buried far away and no one will ever know what happened to her. If the number is even,* Ana continued, *Juan will go away, Monsieur Clive will go away, and we all, Maman, Papa, Rebecca, and me, we'll take the car back to Quebec City and I'll rearrange my room and I'll tell Matthieu that he's a fool and my teacher will be Madame Arnaud and I'll get a computer for Christmas and Maman will bake the cake for my birthday and I'll be eleven and I'll be able to stay up till any time I want. But,* Ana began to count, *if the number is uneven I'll die.*

Just before the end of the boards Ana stopped. She closed her eyes. She didn't want to know.

Staff Sergeant Maurice Clive of the Quebec Sûreté was speaking to Corporal Horace Tremblay at the Percé police station. They were sitting in a shabby little office painted pink. On the wall was a calendar from the Chinese laundry with an Oriental girl hiding behind a fan. *This room is like the interior of a massage parlour*, Corporal Tremblay was thinking. The two policemen were separated by a high pile of dishevelled folders.

Each wanted very much to impress the other. Monsieur Clive wanted to be regarded as the man in charge and used his French from France to great effect. Corporal Tremblay, in order to appear the more knowledgeable of the two, accentuated his Gaspésien accent, opening his vowels and punctuating every other word with a "t".

Monsieur Clive lifted the top folder.

"Bill Bernstein was in the Argentine from 1974 to 1977. His passport says he was born in Baltimore. He's forty-eight. He's on the board of Harcourt Instruments and is supposed to have some sort of a degree from Harvard. Business management."

"Any connections with the Argentine government?"

"None we can trace. But you could hardly be an American businessman there in the seventies and not have connections."

"If you say so."

"Now, it's fairly certain that the other three belong to this group, whatever its name is. It's been confirmed. Officially."

Corporal Tremblay pulled out a pen and started doodling on the Bernstein folder.

"But what exactly do you think they'll do? Shoot him down? Booby-trap his car? Push him off a cliff? They don't look the desperate type. Have you seen them?"

"Round and about. The girl looks depressed, one of the men looks frightened."

"What else do we know?"

"Not much. The quarry they're after is supposed to have

been a military instructor of sorts, a kind of professional torture trainer. Any experience of torture in your section?"

Corporal Tremblay stopped doodling and stared Monsieur Clive in the eye. He had drawn a couple of intertwined birds, their necks sprouting from a common body which in turn seemed to divide itself into several pairs of legs.

"Torture?"

"Of course not. You dyed-in-the-wool Québécois are fortunate not to have had an Algeria, an Indochina. You're a bloody Peace Corps up here. The Red Cross."

Corporal Tremblay said nothing.

"All the do-gooders in Paris pointing their fingers at us. 'Clean Algeria, but don't get your hands dirty.' 'Democracy without torture.' Of course we knew it was happening. We all knew it was happening. Some of the best methods of torture were invented during those years."

Corporal Tremblay grunted.

"And not just by our side, let me tell you. I once saw a boy the *fedayine* had caught alive. Do you know what a bunch of raw nerves looks like, pulled out from under a muscle?"

Corporal Tremblay said he didn't. He put his pen down.

"Not everyone is capable, of course. We had some big, stubborn brutes in our division, and I imagine one or two of them were none too gentle when it came to asking questions. One night the colonel ran off a list of the things you can do to live flesh. By dawn he hadn't finished. You don't need much imagination, you know."

Corporal Tremblay made an attempt to rise from his chair.

"That's what they're looking for, and this is what we're looking for. And information about his alleged torturing activities is not bound to be in Mr. Bill Bernstein's curriculum."

Corporal Tremblay sat down again.

"So we simply keep an eye on our Latinos. Who they see, what they do, when they do it. And if anything seems odd, we grab them. But nothing else before we have proof."

Corporal Tremblay picked up his pen and encased the two birds in a rococo cage.

"Then our business is to prevent a torturer from being killed," he said.

Monsieur Clive stood up and pulled the folder away from Corporal Tremblay's pen.

"No. Our business is to keep the peace."

And then he added: "I'm going down to the motel where the two men are staying, and ask a few questions. We've waited long enough. You can show Monsieur Berence the Bernstein file. Bring him here. See if he remembers having seen him in any official capacity."

Without leaving his chair, Corporal Tremblay watched Monsieur Clive straighten out the pile of folders on the desk so that they were perfectly in line with the edge of the formica top, and then reach for the door. As he did, Monsieur Clive's sleeve caught the top file and a shower of paper floated around the room, covering the floor. Corporal Tremblay waited a full minute before helping Monsieur Clive put the folders together again. As he picked up the sheets, he couldn't help thinking how much he disliked the freckled hands of his superior.

Even as a boy, Corporal Tremblay had looked up at the

blue-shingled house with a touch of envy. It had not always been blue-shingled: once it had been painted red by a man from Connecticut, and another time black, the colour of choice of a certain French lady known to the town as Madame La Duchesse — this when the corporal was eight or nine. She had been brought to Percé by a Montreal gangster, and kept in the big house overlooking the sea, with bodyguards to watch over her, and she had made them wear eighteenth-century costumes and wigs. And Corporal Tremblay remembered the sight of a Versailles procession — the white-wigged and brocaded bodyguards, La Duchesse following their trail — descending the road from the house to the town, one winter, against a grey sky. La Duchesse had died, and the house had been sold, and the new owners had restored the blue to the shingles. If Corporal Tremblay could have had one wish granted, it would have been to possess the house on the cliff.

Of all the occupants he had known, Corporal Tremblay preferred Monsieur Berence. He enjoyed the old man's manner, he liked how fittingly it reflected the nature of the house. *Monsieur Berence and the house lend one another meaning. They suit one another*, thought Corporal Tremblay.

It was just after 2:30. He was driving Monsieur Berence back to the blue-shingled house. "A plot to make me late for my nap," the old man had joked. They had spent an hour at the station discussing the activities of Bill Bernstein. But, as Monsieur Berence himself had warned him, there was little the old man could say about someone he had only just met. Yes, his experience of South America could help him understand some of Bernstein's activities, but how could that lead Corporal Tremblay to identify what Monsieur Clive called "the quarry"?

Corporal Tremblay had laid out photos of Bernstein in Argentina: photos of Bernstein shaking hands with men in uniforms, photos of Bernstein standing in small crowds, photos of Bernstein alone. Monsieur Berence recognized certain faces, certain buildings. But he had never, he said, seen Bernstein while he had lived there.

Politely, Corporal Tremblay had insisted:

"Monsieur Berence, I'm sorry. But you must have seen him sometimes. You say you were at this dinner — Bernstein was there too, for instance."

But Monsieur Berence had patted Corporal Tremblay on the shoulder and smiled and shaken his head.

They drove back in silence. Monsieur Berence looked tired. In a few more days the family would be moving back to Quebec City and the trees would turn brittle and the air would become cold and Percé would be empty again.

Corporal Tremblay thought of winter.

As they took the last turn before the ascent, and the house with its blue roofs rose in front of them and disappeared behind the overgrown hedges, they heard an explosion.

Later, recalling what had happened, Corporal Tremblay realized that for a few seconds he had thought the explosion had been a sound of the sea, an impossibly louder wave breaking against the rocks, or thunder echoed somehow in the water. It took him a moment to see, as they turned into the driveway, that the house had changed. The right wing gables had disappeared, and smoke rose from a black gash in the roof, and there was fire underneath the smoke.

Monsieur Berence leapt out of the car and ran into the house and up the stairs. Corporal Tremblay overtook him before he reached the master bedroom. The upper floor was full of smoke, and they could barely see the bedroom door.

Corporal Tremblay stepped forward to stop Monsieur Berence but the old man had already entered the room. A fit of coughing brought tears to the corporal's eyes, and in a haze he saw Monsieur Berence drag a body out of the smoke.

"Please help me. I can't lift her."

Corporal Tremblay took the body by the legs while Berence held it under the arms. With difficulty, because the legs seemed to slip away from Corporal Tremblay's grasp as if they were fish, they carried it down the stairs and out into the garden. They laid her down on the grass.

With the exception of the face, the woman's large body seemed alive. There were hardly any ashes or bloodstains anywhere on her arms and legs and dress, only charred pieces of what looked like torn-up photographs. But her face had been erased as if ripped off by a monstrous claw; there was nothing there except a gaping hollow.

Corporal Tremblay watched Monsieur Berence as the old man tried to embrace the body somewhere, somehow, and failed, as if the absent face had taken away the sense of the body, had transformed it into something that was not a body, a northless compass which the old man turned and turned in his hands, unable to find a beginning or an end. To Corporal Tremblay, Antoine Berence looked like a man who had suddenly gone blind.

Corporal Tremblay pulled off his jacket and covered the enormous wound. The blue cloth darkened. Then he caught Monsieur Berence by the arm.

"Please, come away."

They heard sirens. Percé's small fire engine and the local ambulance drove in along the laneway, followed by Monsieur Clive in a police car. Doors slammed, men ran into the house, shouting. Two attendants opened the back of the ambulance and pulled out a stretcher. Berence watched them lift the body of Marianne.

Monsieur Clive was by his side.

"Antoine, old man, we'll get them. They won't go far. The bastards."

And then, putting a freckled hand up to Berence's face: "I'm sorry. I'm really sorry."

Berence took Monsieur Clive's hand and moved it away from his cheek.

Monsieur Clive added, for his corporal's benefit: "They stole the motel owner's car. We'll stop them before they reach Ste-Thérèse."

A shout made Berence turn. Ana had just apppeared at the entrance to the garden and was staring at the body on the stretcher. She lifted her eyes and saw him, and ran to him, panting. He put one large arm around her.

A low rumbling clogged Berence's ears, and his sight felt blurred, as if a heavy cold had come upon him all of a sudden. Vaguely, he saw the attendants load the stretcher into the ambulance and close the doors.

The ambulance drove off. Two more police cars arrived, and Berence wondered how they had been able to negotiate the lane with the ambulance driving past them. He put his hand on Ana's head.

Berence noticed that Monsieur Clive was speaking to him. He only caught the last words:

"Go sit on the bench, old man. I'll ask the doctor to give you something."

Blinking to clear his sight, Berence watched Monsieur Clive enter the smoking house. Then he turned his eyes away.

People had come up the laneway and were trying to get into the garden. Two or three policemen were inefficiently trying to push them back. Berence told himself that he would have gone about it differently. He looked down at Ana and wiped her cheeks with his hand.

"Is Maman dead?" Ana asked.

Berence nodded. He had difficulty breathing.

"She can't be dead," Ana said. And then, her voice breaking: "What are we going to do now?"

Berence couldn't talk. He held her hand and walked past the policemen and the people. Corporal Tremblay called out his name, but he didn't stop. Together they walked down the lane to where his car was parked.

"Don't be afraid," he managed to say.

He got into the car and opened the door for her. She climbed in, serious and sniffling. He touched her face, once, and started the engine. As they pulled out of the driveway he turned to her and said: "I'll try and explain."

And then, very gently: "Make sure the door's properly shut. And do up your seatbelt."

Berence drove through Percé, careful not to exceed the speed limit, and then faster along the coastal road.

THERE

ALGIERS

ONE SUNDAY — it must have been in October because the rains had begun — on the hill behind the house, near the riding-stables of Ain-Taya-les-Bains, a thirteen-year-old boy was set on fire by his friends. The boy was French, the son of a local bricklayer; his friends were young Algerians. They had known one another for years, and used to hunt pigeons on that same hill throughout the fall. In his declaration to the police, one of the fire-setters explained that the French had murdered many Arabs, and therefore it was his duty to kill the French in return. Because he himself was only thirteen, he could not attack "one of the big ones", and so he had suggested the French boy as their victim. When asked whether the French boy had not also been a friend, the Algerian boy said yes, and only a friend would have trustingly accompanied them up the hill to where the murder took place. When asked whether he knew what death meant, the Algerian boy said yes, he did know what death meant. It meant something was finished.

I didn't hear about it till the next morning, at breakfast, when Papa looked up from the paper and read us the report.

"Marianne," he said to me, "the world is no longer a pretty place."

I have never forgotten the burning, not because of its horror (it was in itself neither more nor less horrible than other events that took place during those years) but because I had dreamt about it the night before, before I even knew that it had happened. I saw, in my dream, the small figures climbing the hill after the last cloudburst; I saw them against a brown sky, marching towards the top; I saw them gather around one of their lot (nothing distinguished the victim from his executioners); I saw them pour a liquid from a bottle and strike a match. Then I saw flames: no longer a human group, but a dazzling burst of red and blue light casting shadows on all sides. All this took place in silence, as if I were watching a film with the sound switched off. In my dream I wasn't frightened. The fire seemed somehow natural, like the sudden absence of rain.

Now I know how curious it was, not being able to tell anyone, but it didn't feel that way then. I couldn't because I had no one to tell, no one I could speak to without feeling that I was climbing over forbidden fences, entering uninvited gardens reserved for private contemplation. So serious they seemed, too, all those euphemisms, all those niceties. What could be told, what couldn't. The dressage of language. Tricks of the tongue.

Much earlier, the year of my first brassiere — which Mamma had chosen, somewhat embarrassed, at Au Bonheur des Dames — one Friday night at the Milk Bar, Monique had said: "Don't tell me everything. It's not polite." I never forgot her warning.

First the differences. That was what Papa had pointed out when he introduced us, both of us seven years old, I in the itchy grey dress, Monique in her white bows. Monique had been born here, in the very crown of Algiers, sprung from the brow of the city. "And you, my dear," (this to me, the stranger from Lyons) "you will always be a foreigner." Monique taught the foreigner necessary rules. What was allowed, what wasn't. Vocabulary.

When we both turned twelve Monique's family moved from El Biar down to the European quarter, to a big and ugly building that had once been occupied by an Italian mattress-maker. Monique's room had lime-green shutters that were always closed but through which you could hear, day and night, the rumble of the street below, and we would lie on the tiles of her floor — mint and white tiles whose design, when seen from above, wove a complicated wreath of leaves and stems, but when seen from close by, face down on the mineral coldness, became a simple pattern of crossed triangles — discussing what I had learned.

"If a boy holds your hand like this, fingers like a spider: What do you do?"

"I draw back."

"He holds you tighter."

"I get angry."

"He puts his arms on your shoulders. He looks you deep in the eyes. He lets one hand crawl slowly down towards your breasts. He slides two fingers under the strap of your dress.''

And Monique would roll round and lie on top of me, heavy except where her hands grazed my nipples, till she seemed to grow, flow over the sides, her weight too much for me to bear. I'd heave her off and we'd laugh, stretched out on the tiles. Monique's hands too would enter my dreams, but that was to be expected.

Expected or not, I always dreamed with a purpose, a port. I had the ability of fashioning my dreams into deliberate shapes, of blending memory and invention, and I was able to colour the past in my sleep. Not always, but sometimes. I wanted to remember things as they ought to have been. As I wanted them to be.

Shortly after moving to the new house, Dr. Vincennes, Monique's father, invited us to a weekend place they had rented by the sea, at Ain-Taya-les-Bains. For several nights before the date of departure I dreamed carefully of the house, the layout of its large, cool rooms where veiled servants made mint tea, red sand lapping at the doors. It wasn't like that. It wasn't like that at all when we arrived down the tarmac road, filth on both sides, gangs of scrawny cats hunting angrily through the rubbish behind the Hotel Tamaris. It was a red bungalow next to the bricklayer's house, with small windows and a wooden veranda, one single palm tree bending its trunk to the wind at the further-most corner, and behind it all the sea. Mamma visibly sniffed as she got out and stood a little undecided by the car, but accepted Dr. Vincennes' hand to guide her towards the cement path. Papa carried the luggage, putting on an Arab accent, pretending to be Dr. Vincennes' servant, bab-bling away at Madame Vincennes, making us laugh. Of my dream, the only successful passage was the coolness. That, and the scent of mint tea.

We had been told that on the next day, Mamma and Madame Vincennes would take us to see the small Roman ruins because Dr. Vincennes was expecting a few friends. "Men's business," he had explained apologetically to Mamma. "Some Arabs." As we were about to leave, a car arrived. Before we were hustled off, I saw three men in gleaming white kaftans get out and greet Papa and Dr. Vincennes. One of them turned towards us and nodded.

Almost fifteen years later, when Monique was married and living with her husband (whom she referred to only as "the Castlekeeper") and three daughters in Dellys, and I was driving the old Citroën down the eastbound coastal road on my way to see her, I passed once again through Ain-Taya and saw the white façade of the Hotel Tamaris. I thought then, as I do now, how everything I remembered, and therefore everything I knew, was cut into small still snapshots. The pictures I was later to take changed as the years went by, grew sick with experience. But these memory shots neither shifted nor aged, motionless in space and time. Fifteen years later Ain-Taya was still the few sad houses by the sea, and the hotel, decking itself with white wooden lacework and blue lights buzzing with flies in the cold seaside nights, had not grown floor after floor to accommodate travelling businessmen, nor crumbled wall after wall into the sand, but had preserved its old age like something cursed with immortality. Monique was always thirteen or so; Papa and Mamma were in their fifties, both dressed in white, always seen from below, from the great depths of a seven-year-old child; my Algeria was embedded, like an insect in amber, in one early May morning, the night air not yet warm, pink light on the trunk of trees and on the whitewashed walls, the high voice calling the faithful to prayers. But I, my face, the creature trapped in a picture frame, was — is still today — uncertain. Perhaps it belongs to that time — was I fourteen, fifteen? — when Dr. Bencherif caught sight of my eyes in the mirror — that is, if that moment ever happened, if it is not a mingling of moments that took place at different times in different rooms, some awake and some in dreams.

Dr. Bencherif was Fatima's father, but this was private information. We played with Fatima at school, Monique and I, as we did with the many Arab girls in white cotton dresses and black braided hair, with mysterious markings on their fingers. We chanted skipping rhymes in Arabic, eyes blind under a scarf, and gossiped with one another in the brick-coloured yard, and put curses on the teachers. But we were, we remained, French. After school all acquaintance stopped. If we saw Fatima or one of her friends in the street, in a store, we would nod, smile under Mamma's or Madame Vincennes' wary eye, and walk on.

In my dreams, when Dr. Bencherif spoke — his brown face creasing into a smile, the black moustache hiding the upper lip, the tongue moving slowly behind the teeth — not only words came from his mouth. Other sounds would seep into the space behind my eyes: the sound of wind, or the howling of stricken animals. Later, during the demonstrations in the streets of Algiers, the air would suddenly fill with that same kind of noise when the women, faces veiled, black kerchiefs over their heads, broke into a long whimpering howl that could, it was said, drive the soldiers mad. The first time I heard the howling was in Ain-Taya-les-Bains.

That evening, when we came back from the excursion to the Roman ruins — Mamma with a migraine and Madame Vincennes with a twisted ankle — Monique suggested that we walk up to the hotel and watch the people getting ready for dinner. According to Monique, the young waiters undressed in a large room in the back, and from the yard you could see into their window. This, Monique said, was how I would learn about the bodies of men without indecent behaviour.

We crept around to the back of the hotel, through piles of dug-up earth and broken stones. A sickly yellow dog followed us. Monique threw a brick at him, but he didn't run away; he looked up and then lay down, panting, in the rubble. Monique led me on. Inside, the orchestra struck up a waltz. The sky was black except for an orange streak in front of us, and the same orange light burned in each of the rectangular windows of the hotel's back rooms. In a lower one, as Monique had said, the boys were undressing. They were laughing and shouting and pulling on starched white coats over their thin brown chests. Then we saw Fatima.

She was sitting only a short distance away from us, on one of the piles of rubble. In the dark, we hadn't noticed her; only when she turned, a strip of light from one of the rooms outlined her white dress and made her teeth glimmer. She called us. Monique put her hand out to me, demanding silence. "The Arabs don't know about sex, only about having children," Monique had told me. "They rabbit-breed." Fatima would misunderstand our interest in the boys.

Fatima was waiting for her father. She didn't mind sitting on the rubble. He had told her that the visit would be long;

she had spent the day on the beach and wandering through the hotel. At the sight of Fatima, Monique grew unexplainably moody. She insisted that she was hungry; she argued that we should be getting back for dinner. Meeting Fatima had taken the fun out of the excursion; now she was angry. I said I would stay. Fatima and I walked away, towards the beach.

Nights in Algiers were never silent. In the milky darkness dogs would bark, children shout, trees sway, the sea slap against the rubbish on the coast, and unidentifiable sounds would burst through the habitual ones, odd sounds like snatches of organ music, kettle drums, snapping branches, the mumble of frenzied voices, sighs. As Fatima and I stood on the cliff's edge, the wailing started.

Fifteen years later, leaning back against loud silk cushions in the living-room of her house in Dellys, her daughters' voices coming in from the garden, the Castlekeeper's round face looking sternly at us from a silver picture frame, Monique reminded me of that night at the Hotel Tamaris. She had sulked all the way back, she had refused to answer Madame Vincennes' questions, she had gone straight to bed wishing they'd go out and find me and give me a beating. Next morning I overheard Madame Vincennes — who never liked me — tell her that she wasn't allowed to see me any more, and throughout the drive back to Algiers nobody spoke, nobody except Dr. Vincennes, who seemed unaware that anything was wrong and kept insisting on the beauty of the scenery.

Farther along the cliff, a short distance from the lights and music of the Hotel Tamaris, was a cluster of huts, the source of the wailing. Fatima refused to move so, leaving her on a pile of rocks above the slope, I walked up to the huts, which seemed somehow too small for human habitation. A cloth hung over what appeared to be the entrance: I lifted it and stepped inside.

A group of Arab women, faces covered, were sitting on the floor in a circle, swaying back and forth to the rhythm of their wailing. Behind them, a person draped in black was stoking a kitchen fire. And in the centre of the room, lying on a blanket, was a woman. Her dress was pulled up over her stomach. Her legs were parted. A man was bent over between them. The woman screamed, the wailing rose. The man lifted something shiny and dropped it into a basin. His hands, his kaftan, the blanket, the woman's legs, were covered in blood. Then he turned and looked at me. I let the cloth fall and ran back up the slope.

In the dark, walking back towards the hotel, Fatima told me about her father. Dr. Bencherif was a "purifier", a "restorer of the flesh". She was proud of his title. His business consisted of tearing out of Algerian women the bastard children of French soldiers. "It would have had no name among us," said Fatima. "It would have been a ghost. No name, no blood, no shadow. It would not have been French, it would not have been Arab." She said her father threw the bastards to the dogs.

I looked back and saw Dr. Bencherif standing in a triangle of light outside the huts, washing his hands. The wailing had stopped.

Then I remembered a dream: I was swimming at night in the middle of the sea. There was a humming sound around me — much like the wailing of the women, only dimmer — and to avoid it I plunged my head under the water. As I did so, in spite of the darkness, I realized that the sea was made of blood.

I remember this: a narrow cobbled street, balconies leering over it, walls leaning towards one another. The sweetish smell of rotten fruit. Figures in white sheets rustling to and fro. Many voices speaking at once, the speakers hidden. I'm fourteen. We are celebrating peace, the first day of peace. At home, in "the good France", as Papa calls it, war is over. The Germans have surrendered, those Germans whose bombs sometimes fell on a street corner, changing for ever the place of a certain memory, the house where Signora Colombiani lived, the store where Papa bought his tobacco. Papa, Mamma and the Vincennes have come out into the streets to wave handkerchiefs. I've walked away. The tri-coloured flags are hung from the windows of the boulevards, and from here, in a narrow frame at the end of the street, you can see them fluttering in the wind. There is also a sprinkling of other flags: blue with red lines bursting from its centre, red and white clustered with stars, red with a stubby cross. A military band goes by, blaring circus music. An old lady with dyed orange hair comes up to me and pins a white rose onto the strap of my dress, white for peace. I stand in front of a baker's shop, an open cupboard lined with tiles. A wizened man, head swathed in a white cloth, watches over a rack of long thin loaves. Later, when those same thin loaves appeared at my breakfast table in Paris, they would seem to me as foreign in France as myself.

Something bursts behind my ears. Someone has been shot. I turn around and run.

Then I see Dr. Bencherif, standing at a corner with some other men. He asks me, in Arabic, where my parents are, why I am not celebrating with them. As I answer — my

Arabic is not very good, my tongue trips on the words as if I were too shocked to speak — I look down to his big, black-rimmed feet and the dusty hem of his kaftan, and then up to his face. I stand close to him, pretending I am frightened. I remember his hands in the hut by the beach. I want to feel his body under the cloth, which I imagine like sand under water.

Dr. Bencherif tells the men that he had better take me home. As we move away I ask him if we couldn't stop a moment at his surgery, which I know is around the corner. Fatima has pointed the place out to us many times. I think of Fatima, her long black hair braided, and Fatima's mother, always veiled when men other than her husband are around. I think of Fatima's fingers, dyed the colour of cinnamon, clutching Dr. Bencherif's arm, as I do now, speaking to him.

I know that, like Papa, like Papa's friends, like Dr. Vincennes, Dr. Bencherif will not really listen to me. At my parents' house, when Papa or one of the other men talks, they listen. Sometimes they interrupt, sometimes they won't let the speaker finish, but they have heard him and they interrupt because they have heard him. When I or Monique or Mamma ventures to say something, everyone carries on talking, doing whatever it is they were doing before, as if my voice were nonexistent, a ghost of a voice, something that the living, the men, cannot sense. "Women's intuition," Mamma often suggests to justify the wonder of the men on the rare occasions they notice that we have been saying something. "Women's intuition," Papa proclaims then, "makes them the stronger sex." Women's intuition, I say, is simply listening.

When I read a book it is a different book from the one

Papa has read. He calls my reading "an amusement" and says I am lucky not to have to concern myself with deeper meanings. "She reads Balzac as if it were a romantic adventure," I heard him explain to a neighbour who had seen me curled up on the front step with *Les Illusions perdues*. "There is no harm in that." He never concerned himself with my reading except once, when he caught me reading Colette one day after school. He took the book away — *Chéri*, I think it was — and said the only place fit for it was the garbage. And he added, in a kinder voice: "Later you'll understand."

I am determined to make Dr. Bencherif listen to my voice, to the sounds I make, to the words built by those sounds, to the dark and terrible notions that are formed by those words. If he listened, if he realized what prodigious beasts my mind has created for him, he would give in, untie himself, understand. We are at his door. I ask him if I can come up.

The children who come running out of the dark, cool hallway don't care; the masked women in flowered dresses, shelling peas, don't care; the cats, the omnipresent and ravenous cats licking for the hundredth time the empty tin tipped from the rubbish heap, certainly don't care. I follow Dr. Bencherif up stairs that smell of urine and cardamom, and the scents mingle with mine, a warm and early scent as if caught between slept-in sheets, a scent to which I wake and in which I bask, all to myself, every morning. There is nothing I want more than for him to breathe in my scent.

His surgery is a small office lined with bookshelves overgrown with books and papers. A rug hangs over the only window. On the cluttered desk are two marble hands, larger than life, erect, reaching upwards, held together by a growth of stone. He steers me towards his wooden armchair, offers water.

I try to make him sit and talk, but he is listening for something outside, downstairs. Not my voice.

This is how I remember him: Dr. Bencherif is standing by the window, pulling aside the rug to look out into the street. Patterns in the rug's design follow lines embroidered on his kaftan, drawn on his face. He can read the events that become chapters in history books. He'd be able to tell, if he were alive now, why that date was significant, why certain happenings acquired boldface titles on the front page of newspapers. He doesn't see a boy running down the street, a group of men going into the third house from the corner, a woman carrying a basket and walking in the other direction. He sees, as if printed on the pages of one of those history books, the declarations signed and dated, a place in the desert called Sétif, names reeled off as in an index of streets: Ahmed Ben Bella, Ali Mahsas, Mostefa Ben Boulaid, Belkacem Krim, Omar Ouamrane, Lakhdar Ben Tobbal, Mohamed Boudiaf, Mohamed Khider, Hocine Ait Ahmed. He recognizes patterns; he can see, in all its intricacy, the frayed and faded rug.

I can't. Each moment has too many colours, smells, sounds, to be part of any whole. Each moment is an entirety. I try to tell him. But there is an impregnable wall between us, like a large pane of pierced stonework or alabaster, complicated interlaced figures rimmed with coloured marble, and he is on that side, I on this. I can hear him, see him twitch slightly in the dusty sunlight, because the sun is on him, the air carries his voice, his gestures; he can't see me, hear me, I know, unless I open — clothes, arms, legs — everything except my mouth. When I somehow catch his eye, he understands my movements, as I understand the movements of a dog. But not its voice, not my voice. The image shatters. He asks me again if I want water.

The day he was arrested — Papa told us the news as if ashamed, as if Dr. Bencherif had insulted him — I almost asked to be allowed to visit the prison. Ten years had passed. I wanted to remind Dr. Bencherif of that afternoon in his surgery, how he had growled at me to get dressed as he let the men in, and didn't look back as I left. I wanted to know what he had told them: had it been, in his words, his feat or mine? Had he explained, as he was adding paragraphs to that week's history chapter, how the French girl had come to his room? Or had he used the passive voice — had I been brought, been lured, been coaxed, my silence taken for granted?

This is what happened.

By the bed, which was covered in dark rugs and rough square cushions, was a small mirror in a tin frame. I leaned back and stared into it, and I saw Dr. Bencherif looking at me, at my eyes, in the mirror. At last I saw what he saw, and I moved my face so that it was exactly as I wanted him to see it.

I hadn't undressed — he hadn't allowed me to undress. But it was I who guided his hands, put my lips to his neck, sat back on the bed, spoke as he let himself be pulled up beside me. I wanted to discover him, lure him into conversation; I wanted him to tell me if he ate only fish, if he sometimes drank wine, if he had chosen his wife or if she had been chosen for him. But then he moved and raised his hand, his left hand, the hand of impurity, used to wash the dead and feed the dogs, that outcast among the members of the body, shitroom of God's temple, up to my lips, for silence's sake. I bled.

Everything took place as if I had not been there. When the men came in, it was all over, and Dr. Bencherif greeted them by the window. Someone had been shot, they said. A nephew, a cousin, they explained to Dr. Bencherif. When did the shooting happen? Yesterday. During the demonstration? *Allah karim!* A group carrying banners. What banners? Banners in French, not Arabic. For them to read. Yes. We must tell them. They won't hear, they never hear. Show them. Force them. Pluck out their eyes. Rub their eyes on the banners. Teach them to see. Who stopped you? Were they many? How many? (The bed, the corner of the room where I waited, the unastonishing blood on the sheets, were invisible.)

The oldest man was telling the story to Dr. Bencherif. It was like this, he said. The mayor asked the marchers to stop. They wouldn't. The mayor asked them to take down the banners. They wouldn't. The mayor had tears in his eyes, and a red face like a calf's, and a thick blond moustache like the beard of a corncob. Then he ordered the attack. One old soldier covered in medals, a Kabyl from Djemila, lifted his stick and tried to rip down a banner. A traitor. A dog. They walked over him. They trampled him to death. Afterwards, the children scrambled for the medals in the sand.

Papa knew a sergeant of police who had been killed during a skirmish in the early days, when the papers spoke of "Algeria the Peaceful". Every Christmas Eve, at the dinner table, Papa would raise his glass of Algerian wine (in those days he was proud of the fact that he served only Algerian wine) and drink to the memory of "good old Arsenault, dead in the cause of duty, beaten like a dog by the barbarians", and mention Arsenault's single medal, won during his stint as a private soldier during the Battle of the Vardar. He would say grace — Mamma listening carefully, head bowed, watching me from the corner of her eye — and thank Our Lord for bestowing upon us blessings denied to our brethren at home. He would nod towards Mamma, who read us out loud, the day the mail arrived, the letters from a cousin in Lyons: "Imagine that, no white bread, the poor dears, making bread out of potatoes, cabbages for dinner, turnips for lunch, imagine that." And in front of us, on the white lace tablecloth bought in Brussels during my parents' honeymoon, servants would lay out the small bowls of cold cucumber soup, the soufflé of ham nestled in brown clay cups, the saddle of Kabyl lamb which appeared on a large white Limoges dish like a gigantic centipede, bony tips sticking downwards like so many scuttling legs, sprigs of parsley tucked around it in a pool of gravy, with clusters of sand-coloured croquettes piled up on either end of the dish. Between courses Papa and Mamma would carefully spoon through a small helping of Cointreau sherbet which I would be allowed, after much pleading, to taste, and after the green salad ("stronger, of course, than at home; they draw the minerals from the earth," Papa would explain) the Christmas log, the long, chocolate-covered spongecake filled with chestnut purée and decorated with cherries which, during the first years of the war, one of the Lyons cousins would send in tall green jars. Sometimes acquaintances of Papa would be invited, once or twice the Vincennes would join us, but whether we celebrated Christmas

Eve alone or in company, Papa would always raise his glass to the ghost of his friend Arsenault. I used to wonder if, when he fell, someone had picked up the single medal. Spoils of war.

In spite of the random violence here and there, I never truly had the sense of being in a country at war. First the German bombs, then those of the others, those of the *fellagha* or, as some said, though we never believed it, of our own men, were part of what happened every week, every day. Maybe towards the end, before the exodus — when we heard the news from abroad, the colony painted in black and scarlet, news about us — there was some sense of the unusual; but otherwise nothing seemed different. It had always been the same. There were things that were dangerous to do, and places that were dangerous to visit. There were good Arabs and bad Arabs. Sometimes people died, hardly ever someone we knew. Birthdays, holidays, the rains came and went.

That was all.

A few times after that mangled afternoon, when I was visiting Monique's house, Dr. Bencherif would be there and he would smile at me in a polite way that I found incomprehensible. Once, after the end of the war in Europe, I saw him at our house, talking to Papa in the study, and there too he nodded at me, and carried on talking to Papa.

Monique was right: I couldn't tell her everything. A truth might become a betrayal, give offence. What I did tell her, a few weeks after that day in Dr. Bencherif's surgery, was that I had decided not to marry, ever.

Monique said I was crazy. If you didn't marry (she knew this for a fact) your innards dried up and your blood became thinner and thinner, till you turned to dust like the shell of a dead beetle. She had known a spinster aunt like that: one morning they had found her in her armchair, crisp as a leaf, and when they opened a window the breeze had scattered her remains to the winds.

Fifteen years later, after I thought she had long forgotten my confession, she remembered, and I laughed with her when she remembered. I realized that, for Monique, that confession had been everything, the entire sum of my experience. Because I hadn't told her more, because I hadn't listed the secret afternoons with the math teacher's son, the weekends in Oran with the Corsican sergeant, the one anonymous adventure, after the Bal du Printemps, with the mint-scented lorry driver from Tunisia, Monique believed that my world had ended there, at the horizon's dip, and that beyond that nothing existed. I allowed her that belief.

Monique had invited for after-dinner coffee several friends she wanted me to meet. "Not really friends," she apologized. "Being married to an army man is like being the mayor's wife; people expect so much from you."

Later that evening, sitting in the garden outside her house, under the pine trees, she told me that the Castle-keeper's mother was a Kabyl and his father a French soldier — or so the Kabyl woman had told the army chaplain with whom she had left the baby. "He's got some of the Arab's violence when we make love," she said in a proud whisper. "But he pursues his career with the vigour of a Frenchman."

"Here we are, the lord and his lady," said the Castle-keeper, clutching unsuccessfully at Monique as she wiggled past him on the way to the kitchen. "I relish our domain. A fair distance from the capital, but what a refuge, my dear. I don't know that we could survive without it."

My party shoes were beginning to feel tight. I took a cup of coffee from one of the servants' trays and sat down next to him. I asked whether his leave was to be a long one.

"Never long enough and always too long, if you know what I mean."

"She won't, Sabouret, she won't." Another army man turned around and patted the Castlekeeper on the knee. "Women always think time's ours to dispose off. They believe work's something we do to get away from the house."

The man's wife intervened, a grin revealing large buck teeth. "You're wrong there, Bertrand. Monique's friend has no experience with men whatsoever. From what I understand, she's practising to be a nun."

Monique, coming in behind a servant who was carrying a tray of *petits-fours*, rushed to my defence.

The buck-toothed woman interrupted her. "Oh, come, Monique. There are no secrets here, no formalities. Your friend must know what you told us about her! Why, surely you have been friends for far too long to mind a little indiscretion."

A large man whom I had not seen in the darkness under the pine-trees leaned forward and shook a finger at no one in particular. "You are all wrong. You are condemning virtue, praising vice. You laugh, but you forget that we must set an example if we want the desert to be liveable one day. Algeria is far from Versailles."

"Speech, Renard! Speech!" yelled the Castlekeeper and his friends.

I still could not see the large man's face.

He continued:

"You are absurd. All of you. You think that because you are active soldiers you see things in all their tints and hues. You think you change things, you settle things. Nothing changes. Nothing is ever settled. That's the fundamental incongruity of our life. We can patch things up, we can comfort, but in the end it is all deception. The tragedy of Algeria is not that we refuse to offer solutions, or even that we offer the wrong solutions. The tragedy is that there are no solutions. We are here, the *colons* are here, the Arabs are here, just as the dirt and the sand are here. And even if we were to leave, nothing would change. Others would offer other versions of reality. And there'd still be eight-year-olds rummaging through the garbage with the cats."

"He receiveth his words from the Old Man himself," the Castlekeeper said. "And Renard was called unto the Lord de Gaulle and the Lord gave Renard the tablets of the law. Renard, give us His Ten Commandments." He choked with laughter.

"Come on, Renard, we're here to learn."

The man called Renard leaned forward again and scooped up a handful of dry pine needles.

"Would that you were," he said, and got up and went indoors.

"You're impossible!" Monique said to the Castlekeeper. "You're always abusing Renard."

"And he keeps coming back for more," he answered, slapping her on the thigh.

I looked carefully at the Castlekeeper. In the moonlight, his face was silver. His large arched nose seemed to be made out of glass, carefully balanced on the fox-tailed moustache that hid his lips. His eyes sparkled. Glass and iron, scrap metal overlooked by Dr. Bencherif. I wondered if his vision of the war was as mistaken as his vision of myself. Whatever he saw, whatever pattern formed itself in his mind, made out of names and dates, causes and consequences — was it as nonexistent as the stout virgin he imagined before him, stocky and sensible, tidy hair, shrewd eyes, socks rolled down over well-worn patent leather shoes, skin untouched by hands other than her own?

I sometimes wonder why the anonymous craftsmen who carved in stone and cut out in glass the images of female saints gave those unassailable bodies the attractions of the flesh. Why illustrate paragons of sensual denial with sensual bloatings under the draperies, fruit-coloured skin, and warm hair and eyes? Incite in order to forbid. And the denial itself, provoking the temptation; a gorgeous apparition, then broken on a wheel, a spiked wheel. The young girl pierced by a gyrating sequence of pointed phalluses. I picture Saint Catherine much like myself: in a square-cut dress, hair tight in a bun, no makeup. The decisions about who touches what would then be hers. A decorous bride of Christ. Is that what the Castlekeeper sees?

Catherine, with a gypsy face, hands clasping a lily, the infamous wheel and a city, presumably Alexandria, in the background, is cut into coloured tiles on one of the dark niches of Our Lady of Africa. She is not one of the popular saints. The Mother of God, above all, has the largest hoard of candles, and the walls are covered with ex-votos giving thanks to the African Mother of God for answered prayers. Everyone here prays to Our Lady.

One of my first images of Algiers, and also the last, is Our Lady of Africa. We drove up from Bab El Oued, through the Quartier St-Eugène, and past the Israelite cemetery, I seven or eight, Papa at the wheel, Mamma in a painted straw hat, hot gritty air blowing in through the open windows, changing into the medicinal scent of the eucalyptus that dot the mountainside. Our Lady is peach-coloured: we came upon her in the setting sunlight, miniature nuns in blue habits slowly walking in and out of her doors. "She will not be mine," I thought, "until I become African." Not the picture-postcard Africa of lions and giraffes — I knew that much already — but intimate with sand, dry wind, houses with tiled floors, luminous blue beetles scuttling under stones into the shade. When we left, on the ship turned towards Europe, I looked back at the white-stained hills and Our Lady glittering above them, radiant in the sun, and realized that she was, at long last, painfully, mine.

Pope Leo XIII, who in 1900 consecrated the entire human race to the Sacred Heart of Jesus, granted to those who took part in Sunday prayers at this, our church, a plenary indulgence for the souls of those drowned at sea. Mamma understood the dispensation to reach not only the dead but also the living, and felt, from the very first Sunday, curiously blessed by the very fact of treading on the church's worn stones, under the dome of gloomy stained glass, in the presence of the Mother of God Herself ascending over an ocean of blue tiles above the invocation "Our Lady of Africa, pray for us and the Muslims."

Sunday after Sunday, kneeling by the latticed window, I would recite my faults to a large fleshy ear which, in the miserly shards of light, became a mouth demanding prayers of atonement, an eye watching over my guilty memory. "*Une parole peut sortir du puits farouche.*" One word.

Before coming to Africa, in a room that must have been in either Paris or Lyons, as a very small child, I dreamed of an animal, hairless as a worm, whose coils would unfold to reveal a single orifice — eye, nostril, mouth, or anus — and whose presence terrified me more than anything I can remember. And through that dream, and perhaps others, or others in which I forced myself to recall this one dream, I would sit, hour after hour, watching it, unable to move, as it opened and closed its toothless maw, winking at me in an obscene and silent language. When I met, for the first time, the priest's ear in the confessional, the horror of my protean worm came back to me and I realized that it did not want to speak, but wanted to be spoken to, to receive, like fodder, my words.

I began to confess every pleasure, every moment I could remember in the week that had passed in which my mind or my body had enjoyed a discovery, a contact. And after each confession, because repentance was demanded, I would carefully reject the source of every pleasure: the window through which the warm air lifted my nightdress would be closed; the quince jam that took away the stale undertaste of bread would be declined; the soft *chemisier* with Brussels lace sent by a Lyons cousin would be stashed away in bags of lavender until Mamma found it and pulled it out and complained that now it would be far too small for me.

Then, all of a sudden, on my fifteenth birthday, the realization came to me that, for the rest of the world, I only needed to be that which I myself chose to tell. I could construct whole crowds of myself in words, or I could erase myself completely by remaining silent. The tongue was my instrument, like a frying-pan or a chisel. I decided to be brave. I chose to starve the beast behind the window. And so, on that Sunday morning, I promised myself that I would never feed that terrible animal again. I remember sitting up in bed and looking up to the small cross behind which Mamma had placed two stalks of wheat on an Easter long ago, and feeling more awake and refreshed than I had felt in a long, long time. That day, and from then onwards, my confessions were mild and conventional, Dr. Bencherif was never mentioned, and the worm disappeared in the dark.

And yet, again and again, I returned to Our Lady of Africa. Perhaps because it never changed, because its colour and smell remained faithful throughout the years of growth and loss and essay, I returned to it as if the unfolding of my life took place around that mountain and its church, the centre of my world, of what I believed to be my world.

There I was, one morning shortly after my thirtieth birthday, when I saw him again, the man from under Monique's pine trees. Of course, I didn't recognize him, not at once. The interior of a church washes away identities. Everyman is anonymous under the gaze of our dying Lord, I heard a priest say, not long ago. I had come back to waste a Sunday and escape the heat. It was cooler under the eucalyptus and the view of the great blue hazy bay far down at the foot of the city seemed to make the day less oppressive. Inside Our Lady my eyes took a long moment to recover their light.

He knew immediately who I was. His face creased into a smile and he motioned me over to his pew. With the exception of a solitary wanderer, we were the only ones in the church.

"Are you well?"

It sounded like keen interest on his part, not a formality. I said I felt fine and only then remembered his name. Renard. He said he had just returned from Biskra. After he reported to headquarters, Our Lady of Africa was always his first stop. The next, a stroll behind the Kasbah. Would I join him? In his battered Mercury we drove down to the peeling arcades with the little stores and green-tiled coffee shops.

We parked and walked. Renard did most of the talking. As we passed under one of the arcades, he pointed up to a shuttered window.

A few years earlier he had taken lessons there, he said — he and a friend who had just arrived in Africa. Their teacher was an old Frenchman from Poitiers who had become a Muslim, adopted the name Abdel Halim Wahed, and married the eldest daughter of an Egyptian sheikh. However, she died shortly afterwards without having given him any children. Renard and his friend studied with him for several years.

I asked Renard if he had become a Muslim himself. He said no; neither he nor his friend had felt they had enough time, enough strength, to learn.

But their teacher had poured his entire life into the faith. He had studied the holy books for many years — in Arabic, of course — and in the mosque it was said that the soul of the Angel Gabriel was burning within him. Often, in the middle of a discussion, he would stand and begin to sway backwards and forwards, chanting unintelligible words to himself, until little by little you began to understand them, and his voice would rise, and his shaking would become more violent. He would be reciting the *dhikr*, Renard said, the ardent repetition of the name of God.

One night, his friend was passing this very building when he saw a red light flickering behind the shutters. By then they had stopped studying with their teacher, but still, from time to time, they would pay him a visit, bring him some fruit or a box of sweets. Renard's friend decided to see whether all was well. He climbed the stairs, knocked on the door, but received no answer. Then he heard the teacher's voice, loud and clear: *"En-nafs jalas!"* — "The soul departs!" The friend pushed open the door. Inside the one-room apartment was no one. On the rug lay a circle of red sand, like powdered rust. That was all.

I said I doubted his friend's story.

Renard said yes, maybe he should doubt it too. Only his friend did not seem like the kind of man who would lie about an impossible thing like that. "Especially, you see, because I don't think he believes there is a God. He isn't a dreamer, and he is certainly not a journalist. He is a military man, a good man who sees the world as a crowded space around him. He is the centre, you understand. The measure of things. We call him 'The Captain'. As in Baudelaire's poem."

Renard continued. "It's a common story in North Africa, you know. The man drunk with God who is literally consumed by his holy passion. The soul takes over, becomes the body. And then it leaves. *En-nafs jalas*. Proof that our flesh is really a mirage."

I asked him if he believed that.

The sun was fiercely white and coated everything with a milky skin. Men — there were no women in the streets —

moved past us, arm in arm, in conversation, suddenly standing still and staring out across the sea. Renard's eyes
seemed tired in the sun. His creased face looked soft. I
wanted to reach out and touch it.

Renard offered to drive me back to my house. I said I
wasn't going home. He apologized and explained that he
had work to do. Was I certain I didn't need a lift? I hesitated;
then I climbed into his car.

Who, I wondered, will love this old, old man, if not I?
Who will watch him, hands on the wheel, grow young in the
afternoon, shine, become exultant? I imagined his room at
the barracks, his tent on the sand, a holiday in France, in
Brittany perhaps, crossing the sea in the early morning. I
reached out and put my hand on his nape. Very gently he
reached behind and took my hand and put it back on my
own lap. He did this kindly, an adult tidying up after a
child.

The Mercury had stopped behind a traffic jam. Two Arabs
had got out of their cars and were gesticulating wildly. I put
my hand on the door handle, told Renard I had suddenly
remembered something, thanked him, and opened the door.

This is where the dream begins: I am furious. I undo the
bun held tight with an invisible net, ruffle up my hair with
my right hand. My face is like the tiles that make up the
face of Saint Catherine. I walk fast, away from the water,
into the little streets that climb the hill. In the open cafés
men are playing dice. When the dice are thrown the hand
remains lifted, palm spread out, as if frozen in a call for
attention. European faces, clean-shaven, noses saddled with

hornrimmed glasses, chins on umbrella handles, bald heads hidden under homburgs or chequered caps. Arab faces set motionless on striped pyjamas, grey kaftans, or black shiny suits. As I run up the streets the heads turn, except one or two. Of those I am afraid.

Through the narrow lanes, past the shops hung with strips of coloured cotton, under the little balconies covered with sheets and blankets, I stumble in a rage. I leave the Kasbah behind me, the city in a foggy shimmer, the port turning red as if the water had been set on fire. High up I catch my breath.

In a small square planted with dusty trees, a few men are playing *pétanque*. I sit on a stone bench and watch. One of them, the youngest, is concentrating on his game. He has dark, curly hair and in his effort to win his black eyebrows knit together tightly, giving him a cat-like expression. I laugh out loud and spoil his throw.

He shouts at me, in Arabic: "You fool! Go away and take your madness with you!"

I answer that I'm not a fool. It is his beauty that has made me mad.

His friends laugh. He looks confused. He hasn't expected me to speak his language. I have embarrassed him.

I get up and walk away, looking over my shoulder from time to time. I see him arguing with his friends. Then he follows me.

Suddenly it's grown dark. The only light comes from the glossy black sky and from a couple of yellow windows. There are no shops here; only houses behind long low walls. In a hidden room, Barbara's raspy voice is singing "Nantes".

He catches up with me at one of the corners. Down below

us, the city is lit up, but here I have difficulty making out his features.

He asks me where I'm going, what I'm doing.

I am not certain how this section of my dream unfolds. Parts of it are made up of sensations on my skin, or the memory of sensations on my skin. Others are smells, a whiff of *chorba*, of saffron. Or sounds, the boy's nervous breathing, the half-heard words of Barbara about train stations and rain. *"Madame, soyez au rendez-vous."* Be there. Be there. I find his hands and lift them to my breasts.

Then all becomes clear. Lights are switched on. From the wall behind us come screams. Shutters are slammed open.

A man shouts, in French: "Whore! In this house, at my table, in front of my fire! The food you cooked is gall! Nothing of yours was ever mine! Whore! Whore!"

A woman runs out into the street, in the middle of a shaft of light. Her shadow spins wildly.

"Whore! Whore! I will make myself blind so as not to see you! I will strip skin off my hands where my fingers touched you! Everything you looked at in my house I will burn! You have never been here, your name was never called here. Whore! Your name is now Whore!"

Her long hair shakes as if she were dancing. The man is wearing a sleeveless shirt that separates his neck from his arms, his arms from the rest of his body.

The boy has not stopped touching me. From my breasts his hands have slid backwards, lifting my underwear, over my buttocks, then forwards again, all ten fingers searching my pubic hair. I step back. He undoes his trousers. In the darkness, he whimpers.

"In the stone orchard," Barbara sings, *"the last voyage, the furthermost coast."*

The man is on the ground now, at the woman's feet, and her arms are no longer flailing in the light. They hang by her sides, exhausted.

"Don't," he asks her. "Don't, don't, don't." What does he want her not to do? Does he want her not to go, not to love someone else, not to listen to him, not to stand there waiting? My boy reaches once again for my breasts. I push his hand away.

I see his eyes looking at me. He wants me to touch him, but I won't. I allow him to wait there, caressing himself, but I will walk away before he has finished. In front of us, the woman standing and the man at her feet don't move.

This is where I choose to end the dream: I leave the way I've come. This time, the boy doesn't follow.

There are certain private acts of which we will always be ashamed. They are small, like lice, and no one knows of their existence except ourselves. Some I confessed, to be purged of them, in Our Lady of Africa; some I never told because they seemed impossible to tell, so meek and terrible were they. One such was the boy whose face I can't remember, standing in the dark. Another was an apple cake my mother had saved for my father, and which I ate, in hiding, one afternoon. A third, something said to Monique on the beach, when she wouldn't do what I wanted. The details vanish. And there was a fourth one, on the afternoon I met the Captain.

The first time I saw the Captain I thought, "What smooth

skin." As if the flesh had been dug out from underneath and nothing lay there between the skin and the skull. He stood outside the door of our apartment, and it took me a long moment before I asked him in, so fixed was I by the impression of hollowness.

Renard had told him to call on me, and he had. He hoped it wasn't inconvenient. He suggested walking down to the port. He had to meet someone at one of the cafés, but it would not take long. Would I come? Out of idleness and mild curiosity, I said yes.

As we sat there, sipping tea, I paid no attention to his colleague. The sun was going down and a small crowd was coming together on the quay, not far from where the fishing boats docked. The crowd seemed excited: fingers pointed into the distance. Several of the men called to their friends in other cafés under the arcade. I told the Captain I would be back in a moment, and crossed the street to join the crowd.

"They have it, look. They are bringing it in," someone shouted. "There, over there."

I peered over the railing. Standing on the edge of their boats, the fishermen were lifting something out of the water with their poles, something large and long and covered with seaweed. Sharks had eaten at its flank, and in the grey flesh there were patches of yellow and pink. One superb dorsal fin remained intact, preserved from whatever ravages the thing had suffered. The Arabs pointed and laughed.

I have never been able to pinpoint beginnings, to recognize them for what they are. I never told the Captain about the dead sea monster. When I returned to the table his colleague was leaving. Apologetically, the Captain asked me to lunch in one of the small fish restaurants that line the sunken alley between the Great Mosque and the port.

During lunch he spoke little, he listened, and I felt less offended. I found myself telling him about Algiers, creating little patterns for his sake, a sampler of images which I had not thought of collecting before. Definition destroys. Never before had I sorted out and labelled my memories, experiences, facts collected about my African home, and in doing it then I felt I was losing a freedom of which I had never been conscious. I was wrong.

He asked me, I remember, if I thought the Algerian *indépendantistes* were right.

Two years earlier, de Gaulle had spoken here, in Algiers the White, and roared out, like a ham actor in Corneillian drama: "I have understood you." The Captain wanted to know if I too had understood the Algerian demands for separation.

I had lived here for nearly thirty years, almost my entire life, and had heard all the tales we Europeans told about the Arabs. In drawing-room conversations, in coffee-sipping evenings in the garden, at the doors of shops on the Rue Michelet, we explained away the uncomfortable strangeness of their sulky looks, their odd movements, their secret familiarities. "Ah, well, you know," and then would follow an apologetic remark about not fully grasping some unseemly characteristic or other. "Ah, well, you know, they have no sense of property — except their own." "Ah, well, you know, they are the laziest people on earth — they deserve the wilderness." "Ah, well, you know — they are heathens." In the French imagination they were like dragons or elves, an unreal and ever-present group with no individual faces. One's own Arabs, of course, were the exceptions, "so unlike the others" — Mohamed who did the garden, or Mohamed who played dominoes at the café, or Mohamed who kept an eye on the beach house during the rainy season. Until something happened — a broken promise, a forgotten obligation, an attack on the farm of someone one knew — and then the litany would rise again: "Ah, well, you know. . . ."

The Captain wanted to know if I had Arab friends. Surely I must have made friends at school? Curiosity? Enchantment? The danger of something forbidden at home? None. The foreigner had remained a foreigner.

All throughout lunch, the Captain spoke about "*ces arabes*". He had a prodigious memory for names, and he would reel off the long genealogies of the Arab friends he had made in barely five years of Africa. He seemed to enjoy collecting facts about people, and he told me this almost unconsciously, as if he were speaking to an Arab, not a European.

After the *patron* had placed a bottle of red wine in front of us, the Captain's voice changed, became softer. He began with explanations, footnotes to his quotes and references to tribal customs; by the time the first dish had been cleared and the *chorba* soup had been served, he had dispensed with any apologies and he was full into tales of family rivalries, heroic feats, ghost stories, and religious miracles, in all of which he had had a quiet, unimportant hand, and from all of which he had learned something more about the people he called his brothers. Rebellion pained him, not as a soldier but as a lover: he felt that the *fidayine* were less criminal than unfaithful. He referred to them as "*égarés*", as "strays".

His broad shoulders hunched over as he spoke; his broad face creased, making him look slightly Oriental — not

Chinese but Malayan perhaps, or Filipino. His voice was soft, even when he seemed excited, and at times I would lose the flow of what he was saying, lulled by his voice and distracted by his large, curiously shaped ears which gave him a sage and at the same time animal look.

He appeared older than he was. Even in his mid-forties, he looked my father's age, but I never brought them together in the same thought. Papa had about him the stiffness of a well-known official — a familiar fixture, a feature in my landscape, growing old and changing imperceptibly as features in a landscape change. The Captain had the vitality of water under his age. Across the table, his eyes and the grey hair brushed backwards quivered incessantly.

A young waiter in a greasy coat removed the bowls of soup. As he did so, his arm caught my glass, half full of wine, and sent it crashing to the floor. Before he could apologize, the *patron* appeared from nowhere and hit the boy in the face with an open hand, cursing him for his clumsiness. Holding his cheek, the boy crouched down to pick up the pieces of glass. The patron gave him a violent kick. The boy kept on picking up the pieces.

"Scum," said the *patron*.

"We have learned nothing," said the Captain.

For a moment I wondered if he would berate the *patron*, but he ignored him, and spoke to me as if the scene we had just witnessed had taken place on a screen or on a stage.

"And we have taught nothing."

He swept a hand across the room.

"Except to obey. We have taught them that obedience is good. No matter who is at the helm. We have taught them to lift their eyes and look up. Now it is us. Tomorrow the master may be one of them. It does not matter."

The *patron* himself brought the coffee. Without as much as a glance in the man's direction, the Captain put a lump of sugar on the spoon and watched it darken and dissolve in his cup.

"There is a short story — a fable, just a paragraph, really — by Kafka. The animal snatches the whip from its master and whips itself so as to become a master. And doesn't know that all this is a dream caused by a new knot in the master's whip. Appropriate, don't you think?"

But he wasn't really asking me.

It struck me then that, throughout the years, I had accepted the judgement of Papa, of Papa's friends, of people like Monique and the Castlekeeper, about the rights and wrongs of Africa. It was as if the entire country had, for my purposes, been a large white house with airy rooms through which a housekeeper with keys dangling from her waist glided noiselessly and severe, unquestioned by all, surrounded by unspoken laws ruling what could and what could not be done, and who was to be punished if those laws were broken, and how. Eating noisily is bad, being silent is good, washing in water that is too warm is bad, looking into a mirror for too long is bad, walking on the inside of the pavement is good, thinking one nice thought before sleeping is good, whistling is bad. The French and loyal Algerians were good. The *fidayine* were bad. "*Païens ont tort et chrétiens ont droit.*" The battle cry of the Crusaders.

I spoke, and he listened, about the things which I felt belonged to me — I may have said "to us" — and which I loved, things that had certain smells, tastes, colours which stood for the world as I knew it and without which the world had no meaning. I recalled the story of a prisoner from Tamanrasset who was sent to a jail in Nîmes and let himself die of hunger and thirst in order to return to the desert of stone he had been forced to leave. He said: "I am blind, I am deaf, my senses are taken from me," but the guards thought he had gone mad and left him to take his life. I didn't want to lose Africa, and those who wanted Algerian independence would take it from me.

I knew that.

I think the Captain's attraction lay mainly in his eyes. The Captain explained things. The Captain listened. His pale, almost colourless eyes never left your face while he was with you. They sought you out and, once they had found you, they attached themselves to you like curious insects, clinging to your skin. The effect was never unpleasant: their touch felt warm and comforting, and lingered after he had gone. Some nights I would wake up certain that his eyes were there, in the same room, keeping me company. If they had an animal quality it was that of the ladybugs the Jewish children on our street called "*moyshe rabeynes*", speckled, rounded drops of blood crawling from finger to thumb and from thumb back to finger, as if they had no wings, nothing to reveal under their shiny domes. One of the children had a pair of "*moyshe rabeynes*" in a matchbox and had trained them to fly out of the box and back to him.

Throughout the meal I almost told him about the impossible sea monster I had seen, but again and again my voice kept going back to the Algeria he wanted to explore through my memory, and his eyes would very gently coax my voice back to an image, a judgement, a fact. There were few facts, many images.

Perhaps because of the power of his eyes, he, the Captain, was a collector of images. He would remember a description almost better than a scene he had witnessed himself, and sometimes he would ask me — later, much later, during the Paris years, or in Buenos Aires — to tell him what we had both seen because he wanted my voice to reconstruct the image for him so as to pin it to his memory better. He was a great believer in words, in the fastening power of words, in the way in which words moulded and defined the shape of things observed. During a time he asked me to keep a journal for him, his journal, in fact, the things he did and said, the things we did together. There was no vanity in this — he was incapable of vanity. Whatever else he may have been or become (though he did not believe in becoming; he said one "was" — that was all), the Captain never appeared to be vain. He took no pride in achievements. Sometimes, however, he praised others. Rarely, because he demanded something close to perfection. And sometimes he found it.

I didn't visit the Captain's living quarters for the longest time. We would meet whenever he was free, mostly in the evenings and sometimes in the very early mornings. I had found a job at the import-export business of Alphonse Legros, a Lebanese Jew who had come to Algeria in the 1920s and discovered a market for cheap Toulouse brocades in Africa, and a hunger for dried Algerian fruit in the foodstores of France. But Legros felt secretly ashamed of employing a woman to do his managing, and he invented gallant excuses to make me leave early or come in late, especially when his clients were due to arrive, clients from Constantine and Tébessa, from Marseilles or Tours, who felt uncomfortable bargaining with Madame le Contrôleur. I took advantage of Legros's delicate sensibility, and worked barely three or four hours a day while demanding not only a full salary but a yearly raise as well. The free time allowed me to see as much of the Captain as I wanted.

I preferred the early morning, when the sun had not yet fully risen and the city looked almost empty and almost clean, and when a small breeze, hardly perceptible, would sometimes move the leaves of the trees along the boulevards. We would sit at round metal tables on the sidewalk next to Legros's office, and drink coffee and talk. I would talk.

It seemed odd that he was a soldier. He didn't behave as I expected soldiers to behave. He liked order, he liked discipline, but he disliked public displays, crowds, parades. And unwarranted violence made him physically sick. "War follows a strategy," he told me once. "But the man who hits his wife in the face, the child who sets a dog on fire, the lunatic who places razor blades inside chocolate bars — they are as inhuman as anything in nature."

A memory:

We are walking down by the port, beyond the fishing-boat docks, along the blocks of concrete that make up the crumbling sea wall. Long sheets of debris wash against the wall, and sometimes up the steps that lead from the water to the road, clinging like offerings to the rusted nails in the concrete. The gulls, hunting for food, call out in harsh, hoarse voices.

We step carefully from block to block, noticing the strange gathering of paper, plastic, cloth, tin, wood, and the gulls swooping down, one by one, behind a large broken piece of concrete. Trapped between the blocks, its paw caught in a fissure, is a cat. It is thin, very small, and almost all we can see of it is its face, which it holds up, snarling, at the gulls. It is black with blood, because every time a gull descends, it pecks at the cat's eyes.

I try to beat off the gulls and pull the cat out from between the blocks, but as I grab hold of it I realize it is dead, a limp piece of filthy fur. I look back at the Captain. He has turned away, and is vomiting into the sea.

He apologizes for his weakness, and says nothing more, but for almost an hour afterwards he looks grey and drawn.

The Captain was older than I was by some ten years but, in a comfortable sort of way, he made me old too. It allowed me to take my time, slow my pace, feel the pleasant weight of my body beginning to sag in the upper arms, around my waist, under my thighs. I watched his creased copper skin lapping around the insect eyes, the white hair cropped like wheat stalks after a harvest, the fine ivory fingers whose tips came together and separated as he listened, and I felt drawn into his age, far from the noise of curiosity and anxious dreaming, to a place where, for the first time, conversation became possible.

He asked me into his apartment almost apologetically, offering me the choice of refusing without seeming to hurt him. Through Renard, who himself preferred living in the barracks, the Captain had found an apartment on the Rue

Michelet, "the Street of the Powers That Be", as the Algerians called it.

An ornate wrought-iron lift took us up to the third floor. The apartment consisted of five rooms, a kitchen, and two bathrooms, and the Captain kept them all empty, or almost empty. In one room there stood a Louis XV bed, gilt and stained lime green; in another was a table made out of two tripods and a plank, and a rickety chair. He pulled up a footstool — the only other piece of furniture — but didn't offer one word of explanation for the meagre furnishing. I didn't ask. There were books on the makeshift table — Camus and Céline and Drieu La Rochelle and Chateaubriand, and Hemingway, I think — but that is all I am willing to remember. We made love, but I will not remember that.

Instead I will remember our first dinner at home, at my parents' place. Mamma seemed angry at the notion of inviting him at all. I think she had given up the idea of my marrying — "At thirty-two a woman has made up her mind," she would say, "and if she hasn't, everyone else has for her" — and the whole exercise seemed to her a waste of time and effort. But she laid out the lace tablecloth from Lyons, and had the maid wash the tall cut-glass goblets, and ordered the cook to prepare a *boeuf aux lardons* "because men like red meat". Papa seemed frightened. I wondered whether he imagined that his daughter, his now grown and obstinate daughter, was comparing her male friends — the few of them that he knew of — to what he had been, to the fool he had become, frail and hesitant and full of aches and clumsiness, something gone wrong beyond repair, a clock damaged by water. I joked with him and spoke earnestly with him, but he had acquired a painful stutter, and when he tried to answer, or interject and do as he had done when I was a little girl — override with his voice my own or Mamma's — the stutter would make him stumble, would delay him, and with tears of frustration he would listen to the voices of others racing ahead of him, leaving him behind. He began to supplant argument with energetic denial; instead of declaiming, of wielding irony and *bons mots*, he would say, "No! No! No!" as sharply and loudly and quickly as his stutter would allow him, and sometimes slam his bony fist on the table, spilling the salt in the glass cruet. "But you are intent on bringing us bad luck," Mamma would complain, and sprinkle some of the salt over his left shoulder, much to Papa's irritation.

The Captain understood Papa's predicament at once. With his eyes fixed upon him, old man to older man, he spoke to Papa as if confirming notions that Papa held. He didn't speak as much as recognize — rephrase, perhaps, for better understanding — lead the talk in such a way that Papa could nod in approval because it seemed to him, and to those others present, that the Captain was merely repeating what Papa had proclaimed. It was a gentle homage, and gracefully done, and I loved him for it.

"That is exactly what we should hear, monsieur. The army's duty is to the Nation, not to the Nation's people. That is exactly true and we should all learn from it, that we are all servants of a greater cause, and in this the army and the people are but pawns. And now, about Italy's place in North Africa, wouldn't you say that they have proven themselves unworthy? You do? I must say, as a soldier I couldn't agree more, and as a student of history I can see you have reflected carefully on the problem."

And Papa would nod, and smile, and the Captain would smile back, never glancing at the shaking hands or the edges of spittle billowing from the corners of his lips. When the *boeuf* had come and gone, and a Paris-Brest was being served, Mamma enquired whether the Captain had had the honour of meeting General Massu.

The Captain answered that indeed he had.

Mamma enquired further if the Captain was going to see General Massu again.

The Captain answered that he believed he would.

In that case, Mamma continued, she would beg a favour of Monsieur Le Capitaine. Would he be kind enough to convey to General Massu that an admirer of his — no need to give her name, a name that would mean nothing to him, and from such an old woman, too (here protestations from the Captain, waved away by Mamma's impatient hand) — had expressed her deepest admiration and gratitude, yes, gratitude, for certain comments he had made publicly regarding the notion of Christian charity.

The Captain answered that indeed he might, and asked if he might be permitted to know the nature of these comments, as he had not come across them in the press.

Mamma informed him that they had been reported in the parish bulletin, edited by Père Martial, and that what General Massu had pointed out was the fact that in the European quarter — she couldn't help believing that the general was referring above all to the French, because the Italians and Spaniards had been demonstrably less guilty of this error — in the European quarter, she said, the interpretation of Christian charity, the noblest of cardinal virtues, had become victim of an abusive and anti-national interpretation.

"We pro-pro-protect our mu-mu-murderers," Papa managed to expostulate.

"We most certainly do," the Captain answered. "I will be proud, madame, to convey your approval to the general."

Mamma's face creased into a smile.

The Captain told me afterwards that it had not all been politeness, that he sincerely liked my parents, and that they held the notions upon which the whole sense of being French, "*être français*", relied. "We require definitions," he said to me that night. "Without them there is no understanding and no achievement. To define is to pare down, to mutilate, to censure, but we are hypocrites if we pretend that we can be anything at all without definitions. That is what is meant by saying that people like your parents are the salt of the earth."

He dabbed at his shirt where Papa had, in an effort to shake his hand, spilled his wine.

Things happen. Innocently we believe that action is a cause, not a consequence; that we could, if we wanted to, advance beyond the last step taken, choose our destination. Algiers. Paris. Buenos Aires.

We got married on August 6, 1961.

Mamma had asked whether we wouldn't get married back in the old country. For months now the rumours of exodus had grown in the European quarter. Private sales of property, signs in shop windows, ads in the papers, announced a letting go of possessions. No one said "we will leave" but everyone knew that our time in Africa was over. The Captain said he understood, but that we would have the ceremony here, perhaps our last accomplishment in Algeria. He said this at the dinner table, where he now had a place almost every evening, except when he had business outside Algiers. Now that Papa seemed too frail even to talk, Mamma deferred most decisions to the Captain — the choice of wine, the household's position on the government's proclamations.

The night before the wedding I slept badly. It had been unbearably hot during the day, and night brought no relief. Mosquitoes buzzed annoyingly behind the gauze curtains, and sometimes got through, too sluggish in the hot air to be ferocious, sticking to my clammy skin. My sheets were wet before dawn, and I got up uncertain whether to change them or simply wait for morning reading a book. I decided I would sit in front of the balcony windows. I walked barefoot into the dining-room.

Papa was lying on the dark carpet. Around him, the room seemed to have been overturned by a fastidious thief. Everything was out of place and yet organized after a fashion. In the shock of seeing Papa on the floor, and the urgency to call an ambulance, I didn't notice that the whole room was a display; only afterwards, waiting for the doctor to arrive, I did understand what the display meant.

The table was laid out with the Lyons lace. A French stamp had been cut from an envelope and Marianne, in her revolutionary cap, had been set up — tiny, disconcerting — against a bottle of Burgundy. Several books had been placed around the bottle, forming a red wall — Papa's collection of morocco-bound classics: Racine, Corneille, Victor Hugo, Daudet. (*Tartarin* had always been Papa's favourite, "our only *pied-noir* classic," he would say.) No Camus: he called Camus "that pretentious journalist from Oran". The French flag — a small replica that had been given to him many years earlier at the chess club, together with a silver medal — was there, and also a blue and white Dubonnet ashtray, and postcards from Brittany and Normandy — a Breton peasant in her costume; a low white cottage in a stony landscape; the rocks of Étretat, which I had never seen, and which many years later echoed in my memory, one morning before summer began.

He had dressed the room with the obvious symbols of France. He had wanted, knowing perhaps that his body and mind were leaving him, to make an assertion that was as much an affirmation as a refusal. He had wanted, suddenly, stubbornly, to be purely a Frenchman; he had wanted to die like something not African.

The wedding was not postponed. The Captain was leaving on an assignment that same night, and Mamma, curiously determined, insisted that we carry on as arranged, while Papa's body waited at the undertaker's parlour. We moved from wedding to funeral as if this sequence had been planned all along, the outfits of the wedding guests became the sober attire of the mourners, and Père Martial, after making a short speech on the duties of married life (his text was from Saint Paul's Letter to the Ephesians), spoke at Papa's burial of St Paul's assurances of Heaven. For a moment I was afraid he might confuse the two.

Only when the day was over, and the Captain had left me and Mamma with the promise that he would be back as soon as possible, and the last friends had said goodnight, and Mamma had whispered that she was going to bed, her body sagging and at an odd angle, as if she had been assaulted with blows to the stomach and chest, and I had turned off the lights in the dining-room, now tidied up again by the routine-loving maid, did I look out on the yellow lights in the hot August darkness, and I thanked Papa for having, in spite of his recantment, given me a sense of place and guarded it for me for so long, until he obviously could hold it no more, until, exhausted and bewildered by politics and history, he confessed his true allegiance and died.

When the Captain returned — we had agreed to live with Mamma in the house that was now hers — he told us that very soon we would be going back to France. "They are speaking of a French-Algerian truce. It is time to leave."

"Papa should have waited," Mamma said.

We stayed on for another nine months, slowly giving up little parts of everyday life. Every time another crate was packed, there were fewer recognizable landmarks around me, as if the very reality surrounding us were disappearing and we ourselves would, at a given point, be devoured by it too.

Mamma refused to travel by plane. On June 17, 1962, at 7:00 o'clock in the morning, we boarded the boat for Marseilles. I stood on deck most of the voyage, looking back. The last clear image of Algiers was Our Lady of Africa, gleaming like a sand castle on the fading mountainside.

PARIS

WHO AM I?

I imagine myself in a hall of mirrors, but every mirror throws back a different face. They are all myself, but which one should I choose? Because choose I must. As if I were required to present a passport photograph, a small square shadow of myself. Which then? At what age? In what clothes? In what mood? How distant from the camera? Surprised or posed?

If I look quickly back, the image is terrifying. A seven-year-old girl running as her head bloats, adolescent face on a short body, body growing, hair styles changing, thirty-year-old torso carrying a small dimpled me, growing old, growing old, years missing. Standing in a white gauze dress, sheet after sheet falling at an angle to the ground, shoulders bare, a white satin rose pinned over my right breast. Dress shortens, tints to red, the rose spreads out in a layered pattern. Now it's autumn. How old am I?

In the summer of '64 — or was it '65? — I found out I was pregnant. The Captain was away on duty, and I sat in our Paris kitchen with the long peeling windows open over the courtyard, and drew up a list:

— *Eyes: dark brown, too big.*
— *Hair: usually too long, black. Never had it cut short.*
— *Nose: fat. It has shrunk as I have grown. Eventually, I think, it will fit my face.*
— *Neck, chin: too plump. Solid.*
— *Mouth: fussy. I have seen lips like mine on Greek vases. Charming, but the effect is spoiled when I smile.*
— *Body: Large, bulky. Except for legs. Legs are slender. A minotaur of a body, animal torso on woman's legs. Body now inhabited.*

Maybe this is the image to preserve. At the kitchen table, defining myself. A mirror in a mirror.

In the hall, as soon as I opened the apartment door, my body was reflected in a full-length looking-glass set in a heavy gilded frame. There was little light in the hall and, especially coming in from the blaze of the street, one could hardly make out the identity of the reflection in front. One knew who it was, who one was, but one's eyes could not quite grasp it. The Captain's fedora always hung there, the ghost of a reminder. This made one think.

The apartment was on a street that has since become a tourist shopwindow; now I am told that the hole of Les Halles has been filled and the area gentrified, and the prostitutes have moved farther north on St-Denis, along the boulevard where the decapitated saint carried his own head on his way to the Martyrs' Mountain.

In summer the city was empty, and I missed him more then, absence upon absence, every other café and store and bakery being closed. The warm air would remind me of home, except when it became too damp, and I would make lists of places we would visit together when he returned. We did sometimes visit those places, and I would jot down their names in the journal I kept for him, but most of the summer I walked about alone. Down by the Goutte d'Or I'd walk past the North African stalls, and see the kaftans and the sandals and the skull caps, but they were foreign here, and I was not, even if some of those foreigners had lived here much longer than I had, because this was Europe, and that was Africa, Gaul and Carthage. Once I tried speaking to them, to a tall Kabyl selling wooden bangles, but he laughed as if I had performed a clever trick. Soon I was nodding to the concierge when she, from Portugal, spoke of "those filthy Moors" who came and set up their trinkets on dark carpets on Étienne Marcel.

I changed so quickly I hardly noticed it was happening. The many-coloured diagram of the Paris Métro replaced the giddy tangle of laddered Algiers streets. Spices mellowed. Food grew tamer, cleaner, pristine in its elegant raw-ness, chicly sparse. The same strong body became lumpy. The skin turned pale. Silence was golden. Introductions were necessary. Distances increased. Cities drew nearer. Weather became blunt. Flowers were expensive. Steak was cheap.

And yet, people I had never known called me sister, fellow exile. Neighbours asked me about poisonous snakes and recipes for couscous. The words *Allergie*, *Algèbre*, *Algues*, sprang up at me from the newspaper pages. And soon I would be offered a seat in the Métro, reserved in priority for: *first*, invalid veterans; *second*, invalid civilians; and *third*, pregnant women. My life among the handicapped.

One evening we invited Monique and her husband to dinner at La Tour d'Argent, overlooking the towers of Notre Dame. She and her Castlekeeper had lost their sharp edges, become diffuse, almost mellow, as if someone had poured them, thick and cloying, over the velvet wallpaper of the restaurant.

The Castlekeeper spoke of North Africa as the abandoned land, relinquished to the wolves and to the desert. Bitterness had taken the strength out of his voice and it quivered a little when he described the chaos he imagined in our homeland. He seemed to have streamed all his energy into eating: he cut huge pieces of *tournedos*, mopping up the blood with bits of bread.

Monique said little. She seemed ashamed of her husband's weakness, and looked at the Captain through lowered eyelids as she moved elegant slivers of veal across her plate. She laughed approvingly at the Captain's remarks, and two or three times declared that he was right, so right. I forget what the Captain was right about. She hardly glanced at me throughout the meal.

The two men discussed de Gaulle. The Castlekeeper grimaced. For him, de Gaulle had brought an end to decency; they had been betrayed, he said, and it was as if their own father had betrayed them. The Captain, who was not fond of melodrama, described a farcical bureaucratic tangle at the Quai d'Orsay.

Monique raised her eyes almost for the first time.

Suddenly I realized that Monique was trying to seduce the Captain.

"We should be ashamed of the example we set for our children," the Castlekeeper whispered.

"Children are not everyone's concern," Monique said. "Marianne is wise. She has chosen not to be burdened."

"Every man should have a child," the Castlekeeper insisted.

"But not every woman can have one." Monique spoke to her husband but glanced at the Captain. "Some women are gifted, others are not. Like artists."

"True," said the Captain, and reached across to hold my hand. It was the only time I saw him being deliberately rude.

Monique blushed and concentrated on her veal.

The Captain and I had not talked about having children. We had talked about other people's children. We had wondered about Diane, the prostitute who had decided to have her baby and who had moved to an apartment below us. We had followed the case of the kidnapped brothers whose mother assured the police that the kidnapper phoned her every night telling her how he was forcing them to forget her. We had learned that the Egyptian-looking fountain outside our building, showing a woman with a pitcher in one hand and a flaming torch in the other, was a likeness of Jeanne de Lorraine, who in the fourteenth century took upon herself the task of setting Heaven on fire and extinguishing the flames of Hell "so that my children will love God for His sake only".

To myself, I had said that I couldn't have children. I didn't want technical explanations. I didn't ask my doctor, or demand scientific reasons. I assumed the fact to be part of myself, not as a failure but as a difference, like not being able to write sonnets, or fly, or remember in chronological order the fifty kings of France.

He had just returned from an assignment when I received the news, and he was delighted. All that night he held me in his arms, as if incapable of falling asleep, cornered in the large bed, listening to the noises from beyond the courtyard. We didn't talk about the child; we simply waited, as if we could sit there waiting all nine months, while police sirens wailed in the streets below and the neighbours' flickering television sets rumbled far away, like the sea.

Another change: from nowhere, stores that sold babies' goods appeared, ads for diapers, rows of baby food in the supermarkets, discounted babies' clothing at the Prisunic. I refused to buy anything yet — the superstition that believes that the future will not take place if we foresee it. Mamma had gone to Lyons to live with the ancient cousins, and I decided not to tell her until later. I'm glad I didn't.

All that summer I spent outdoors, on the bridges, in the parks, down the small streets that surround the yellow churches and the gated gardens. Except on Sunday afternoons. On Sunday afternoons I'd slip into one of the small movie houses tucked away between the Boulevard St-Germain and the *quais*, and watch story after story, a different world from that which had flickered across the large screens in Algiers — slicker, brighter, as if this too, film, belonged to another class, quick and fashion-conscious. *Doctor Zhivago* with Omar Sharif looking like a very young, clean-shaven Captain; Julie Christie as unlike myself as anyone I ever saw; *The Sound of Music* sung in French by a grating mezzo-soprano, *"Do, do-do, endors-toi bien. . . ."* Later, in the movie theatres in Quebec, the rude rustling of popcorn, the slurping of drinks, the crinkling of candy wrappers, drove me away from films. The ones that roll now through my memory are those from far beyond — the earlier, the clearer.

There would be conversations with the other tenants at the apartment house, Diane and her baby boy, Madame Honfleur and her mop-shaped dog, and the older couple whose name I've forgotten, both white and arched forward like Gothic statues in limestone. Once I asked Diane to come with me to the movies, one sweltering afternoon when the air was so humid it was difficult to breathe, but she looked shocked and said no, as if I had infringed on something she had carefully fenced in, or out.

A few times, towards the evening, when I lacked the will to prepare supper for myself alone and the Captain's absence seemed greater and heavier than before — especially when a stray shirt came into my hands, or one of his books fell open on a page he had read me out loud — I'd walk down to the river and across onto the other bank, and down to the church of St-Germain-des-Prés, and sit at the terrace of the Café de Flore. The other café, the one with the two wooden mandarins perched on their high shelves, was closed most of the summer, so it was at the Flore that I would sit in front of a freshly squeezed lemon juice on a green table, my belly still growing, silently pushing as if I were becoming my own double, the shadow of myself.

One Tuesday afternoon (why do I remember so clearly that it was a Tuesday?) a young girl at the table next to mine turned around, excused herself, and explained that she wished to ask me a question.

I looked up from the book I was reading, and smiled at her, a bit surprised.

"When is it due?" she asked, nodding towards my belly.

I wondered how she could tell. There was nothing, I thought, anyone could see. My big body made allowances for space, my summer dress was large.

"It's your skin," she said.

She turned to her companion, a lanky youth with long black hair like a horse's mane, and whispered something to him, very quickly. He nodded.

I thought then: *this is a face I'd like to frame*. I wanted to be able to hold her face inside a square of light, up in the air, against a wall. To inspect it, as one inspects a map. I thought: *if I had a camera, I would take her picture*.

"We're actors."

I smiled again.

She had assumed I too worked in the theatre; something about moving and sitting up in a peculiar way. Her name was Ana (and in my mind I opened a small room in which the name was to be preserved till the right time came) and they were rehearsing a *spectacle*. I told her I was from Algeria — the foreigner, once again. Her face lit up. The play — the vast, as yet unscripted, ambitious play — dealt with war and oppression. I told her I wasn't certain if we were on the same side.

"Oh yes," she insisted vehemently. "We are. I know we are. I can see that in your hands."

Ana explained and her companion — Jean-Noël, the silent Jean-Noël — nodded. While she spoke he played with her hair, which she wore braided down her back, and his flicking the braid distracted me from her words. Ana's play would set on stage a new language of movements; the body would speak, and the words they used would act as music. Ana believed she could read my movements like someone reading a book. Would I come and watch them rehearse?

I said yes.

I paid for their drinks and my own — the first of many times I would pay for their drinks, their sandwiches, their hard-boiled eggs eaten as if they hadn't eaten anything in the past day or so. *Another task of age*, I thought, *the paymaster, sustainer of youth.*

The theatre, they hoped, would be a place on the Boulevard des Italiens, but now the rehearsals were in the back of a tailor's shop on the Rue du Vieux-Colombier, and in the dank, gloomy room Ana and her friends asked me questions and improvised around a story of cruel conquerors and martyred rebels which was translated into jumps, stretches, tiptoeing, and embraces. I would come early and sit in a broad-backed armchair, and watch them shake their arms and make apeish sounds and lie on the floor and breathe in, breathe out, relax, empty their bodies, to be someone else on stage.

Ana explained to them about my pregnancy, but when they asked I had little to tell them, because I didn't really know much about what exactly was taking place inside me: growing, sprouting, bloating, soaking up my food and blood, what? Thinking about it gave the thing inside me a shape, but not much. Perhaps the recognition of a sound, of a form pressing here or there, or was it imagined? Too soon to tell, too soon to know how, what, when.

Ana and I stayed after rehearsals, had lunch together in

cafés or on benches in red gravel parks, went out at night to the Cinémathèque (Ana's discovery, up to five films in a row, each for a franc fifty; the Cinémathèque replaced my little caves near St-Michel, gave me yet another past.)

Ana wanted to know more about the Captain, the best beloved, the absent husband. And there again, I could say less about him than about how his shape, his voice, his eyes, his manner, his talk, his listening to me on and on into the morning, had made marks on me, changed me, allowed me to be at peace again, purged of anger.

I realized that I knew nothing, or very little, of his work. *An office job*, he always called it, and I imagined him at a desk littered with dog-eared files, a filthy ashtray, empty coffee cups. Sometimes he mentioned being called to instruct a group of officers in Strasbourg or Arles or some such place, and I could imagine with what great effort he would confront the stolid faces and try to explain to them whatever it was, his Algerian experience, perhaps, his systems of coping with bureaucracy. *I live in a nightmare of official forms, illiterate memorandums, badly spelled reports, and illegible instructions*, he once told me. I repeated this to Ana and she laughed.

She wanted to hear about Algeria, "where things happened". She imagined North Africa a vast and grubby nightmare, where devils in French uniforms tortured the natives. She wanted to know if I had seen anyone tortured.

The question seemed to me so absurd, I laughed. Ana, wide-eyed as a child, wished to hear about the horrors of Bluebeard's Castle. I told her, truthfully, that I had seen nothing, that there had been nothing to see. Rumours, of course, there were always rumours. I recalled that Papa had said that we, the *pieds-noirs*, would never be victims. Ours was not a defeat but a redressing of justice.

I asked Ana to dinner at the apartment, and we both sat eating roast chicken and drinking wine till it was light again, talking not about the birth or the theatre, but about her, and me, and those bits of history with which each of us decided to portray ourselves. I thought of introducing her to Monique, then rejected the thought. "Is that your new pet?" I could hear Monique ask. "Does she perform tricks? Is she house-trained?"

Ana was twenty. To her, the place I came from was immense, unknown, extending so far into the past that it hurt her even to think about it. Her parents were from Brittany; she had come here to study, supervised by an aunt, and then the aunt and the studies had faded away and the letters from home had diminished. She had met Jean-Noël during an audition. "I took him in like a stray dog," she laughed. "All wet and frightened."

I wrote to the Captain, to one of those addresses that were only his name and a number — it always seemed impossible that letters like this should reach him — and told him about Ana and her group, and he wrote back a letter full of love, encouraging me to work with Ana if I wanted to, and to take care. I put his letter away in one of his books — I kept one of his books by the bed to browse through, and to hear his voice come back as I read the words.

One day, walking down the Rue de Rennes, I saw a camera in a photo shop. I went in, held it for a while in my hands as if it were a shiny black animal, and bought it. (I could never do anything like this when Ana was present; I felt embarrassed at being able to buy the things I wanted, at taking for granted that there was money in the bank. The daily bitter undertaste of not knowing where the next cheque would come from, the urge created by the lack of five, ten francs — these were things I never felt, had never even thought about until my friendship with Ana.)

In Algiers, once, I had borrowed Monique's Brownie and taken pictures of our street, of the next-door neighbour, of Monique in a polka-dotted dress standing in front of the school. None of these photos survives.

The next day I brought my new camera to the rehearsal.

One of the girls was walking back and forth across the room, her arms like semicircles. A young man joined her, then Jean-Noël stepped in. Suddenly all three turned and formed a giant Kali, six arms waving behind the girl's body. She began reciting her lines, a long description of the sea, I think it was, and then stopped and said the words were not working.

Ana turned to me: "Give her words. You want to work with us — find words for her."

I lowered my camera. Two large grey cats left their corner and came towards me. One rubbed itself against my leg; the other strolled away and lay down against the wall.

"*Donner sa langue au chat*," I said. Let the cat have your tongue.

"Go on," Ana insisted.

"With what?"

"Phrases. Idioms. Ways of seeing. That's good. Go on."

I went on.

"Play with fire. Cover with blossoms. Sleep with one eye.

Be like a bird on a branch. Be in the clouds. Take lodgings under the beautiful star. Cost the eyes in the head."

"More," Ana prompted.

"Make the cathedrals dance. Go against wind and tide. Speak with an open heart. A horse with four white feet. Happy as a fish in water. Go through the four hundred blows. To sleep standing up. Look for midday at fourteen hours. Yoke ants to a cart. Be all fire all flame. Loose your head. Cry misery."

The girl started writing my gibberish down. Everyone made suggestions. Two or three times we changed the order of some of the phrases. Then, a couple of hours later, we had a text.

"Try it out," said Ana to the girl. Through the lens of the camera I snapped away at the girl as she moved to the sound of the strung sentences. My first portraits were of this figure whose name I have forgotten, twisting her body into idioms against a background of peeling wallpaper.

For several days the text grew, changed by interpretation, moods, new ideas. I would look forward to the gathering. Before then, every morning, in the Captain's absence, I would get up at seven or seven-thirty — I wasn't sick in the mornings and it would be too hot to stay in bed any longer — and sit at the kitchen table with yesterday's baguette — paler, I thought, than my Algerian ones — toasted under the grill, a bowl of black coffee, delaying the moment of actually stepping out into the street, finding something to do. Not any more. Now I'd be the first at the door of the studio, sometimes waiting outside at a café table, anxious to start.

At first I took my pictures to be developed at the store, where a sultry Belgian would take my camera, perform on it a miniature Caesarean, and then, a few days later, return a contact sheet for me to choose those images I wanted to preserve. The routine seemed to bore him utterly. Only once he said, as I handed back the contact sheet crossed here and there in red wax crayon: "Selective memory. Very nice."

Then I started developing on my own, using the bathroom as the darkroom. With a touch of guilt (I had never spent that much money on something I wanted for myself) I bought an enlarger.

The Captain arrived home unexpectedly. There was little time, he said, to warn me, and I was so often out (this not as a reproach but as a statement of fact) that he had preferred to catch the first available train, rather than wait and be driven in one of the small official cars.

During his absence I had held conversations with him in my head, made lists of things to tell him, explained to him my new occupation, my new friends, reminded by his books every night and his fedora every morning. But when he actually arrived the news summed itself up in a few words, delivered almost at first sight, and then it was as if he had never left. That afternoon, for a few hours (no more), we walked along the streets I had used to see alone, and looked at the store windows I had watched change, and crossed the river by one of the ivory bridges, and then followed the still green water from above, along the quais, from where I had taken a series of pictures which I wanted to show him (but which I kept until his next visit). Alone and with him I decided on different places; for him I chose Île-St-Louis, with its single backbone street running between thin gaunt buildings, and the womblike Place Dauphine, where men in baggy blue trousers played *pétanque*. We listened to a Brahms recital at the Conciergerie.

I liked holding onto his arm. I liked sitting by his side as he placed a big hand on my belly, hunting for movements. I liked him in his silvery summer suit that rustled very slightly. While he was there, the camera stayed at home. Then he left again.

It happened one Friday night. Ana had said she would pick me up at home and we would go and see an *Andromaque* which a friend of hers, Dominique Serreau, had directed. I had never seen a production of *Andromaque* but the verses, drummed into our heads by Soeur Amicale at the Lycée in Algiers, came back like music on odd occasions, and even now certain lines refuse to be forgotten:

"Où suis-je? Qu'ai-je fait? Que dois-je faire encore?"

Indeed — what must I still do?

That afternoon I had felt somewhat nauseated. The heat had rotted the uncollected rubbish piled up outside restaurants and food stores throughout Paris. Here and there a single Algerian immigrant worker in blue swept the gutters with a broom made out of twigs, but it wasn't enough, and the smell of the city, like an overripe fruit, lay thick around everything. Cats, plump, large, arrogant, prodded the boxes and bags, but even they seemed overwhelmed by the pungency, and walked off in search of shade. The tourists were nearly naked, red as raw meat, reeking of butter and American aftershave.

When I reached the flat it was nearly six, but the sky was still as bright as midday and no cooler. As I opened the door and faced myself in the gilded mirror, a cramp gripped me in the stomach. I bent over and closed the door. I stood for a second there, catching my breath. Then I looked down. Behind me, where I had stood, were a few drops of blood. A second cramp, this time stronger, and I felt as if something had loosened itself inside me. My thighs were wet. I put my hands between my legs. Blood seeped through my underwear. The bathroom was full of development trays I had not removed. I ran to the toilet and sat on the toilet bowl. I looked at my hands, filthy from the dirt in the streets, now streaked with blood, and burst into tears.

The cramps disappeared, but there was a dull pain inside me, as if something had hit me from within, bruised me. I could hear the drops of blood falling at irregular intervals on the water inside the bowl, like the aftermath of rain.

The doorbell rang and I called out, hoping Ana would hear me. She shouted my name, once, twice, probably saw the trail of blood, and found me, my face in my hands.

As I gave my name and address at the hospital, I realized that there was no way of reaching the Captain quickly. I could leave messages for him at headquarters, but there was little chance of him returning in less than a day or two. I asked Ana not to call him, and to wait with me. I was given an anesthetic and wheeled away.

When the Captain arrived two days later, I was at home, in bed. Ana had, in spite of what I had asked her, called him the next day, and he seemed hurt, not angry. "I wish you had called me sooner," he said. He sat by my side, on the bed, and lifted the hair off my face.

"Oh strange, strange woman. Big, beautiful woman," he said.

We never talked about the loss. He left the choice of talking to me, and I didn't choose to recall it, as if I had witnessed a miracle impossible to describe. He took, or was given, an extended leave, and when I felt stronger he rented a small car and we drove to the north, to Étretat, where his family's house had been, and where Papa had spent one memorable holiday. We went through ugly little cement villages built after the war, and down to the beach road that leads to the rocks, and we stayed at a small hotel with Spanish arches and bougainvillea and lantanas, and took long walks along the seafront, watching the tourists not rich enough for other summer resorts or too rich to make a change, behind striped canvases that protected them from the wind. In Ain-Tayales-Bains the canvases were red. Blue, I thought — so much more civilized.

One afternoon we sat at the mouth of a huge cave, watching the pierced cliffs jut out from the foam, and he recited Hugo to me.

One word may spring from the hideous pit.
Don't ask what it is.
If the mouth be the abyss,
Oh God, what then is the voice?

This time, his departure was more painful.

He wrote to me, which he had seldom done before, but that seemed to accentuate the absence. I had put his books away in the spare bedroom, because they now seemed like keepsakes of a voice I missed so much, and stored his fedora away in the closet. Ana would visit and complain about Jean-Noël, or about the weather, but the rehearsals had begun in earnest and she didn't have much time. I promised I would go back and follow the play's progress, but it was difficult, because her friends would stare at me guiltily, uncertain if they should offer condolences or pretend to ignore the fact that anything had happened, as if my loss were not quite a loss, midway between an accident and carelessness.

For a time I stopped taking pictures.

The city now seemed larger, its spaces different. I had grown older suddenly, my body wizened. The men who had looked at me lovingly, making me feel ample and beautiful, now looked past me.

I had become transparent. I walked alone.

Then, in the autumn, Ana married Jean-Noël at the town hall of the fifth district. Her parents came for the ceremony, sallow-faced, dressed in brown. Ana had made flower wreaths for herself and Jean-Noël, and a hairnet full of silver stars for me to wear. A group of musicians playing Indian instruments made music outside, on the street.

It rained.

One Sunday, crossing the Jardin des Tuileries from the flat green basins in which the children floated their boats to the small Arc du Carrousel crowned with a god's chariot, I decided I would walk into the Louvre and spend some time among the cool white statues. I walked along the corridor of marble troughs and reclining torsos, mounted the wide staircase under the flight of the headless Victory of Samothrace, her body under the stone clothing as mine had been, full and round and rich. "Mother," I prayed, "give me back my strength."

I climbed higher and crossed the long halls of French paintings, grandiloquent and overcast, and then, in order to escape a group of tourists, turned sideways into one of the smaller rooms. On the southern wall, between two windows, was the portrait of a woman.

It was a small portrait. The woman's head was no bigger than my hand. Her hair was blonde and thick, and cut against the dark background. She was wearing a rust-red shirt or dress; I couldn't tell because the picture ended below her neck, a solid neck, a working woman's neck, the colour of ivory, like her face. It was her face that held me.

Her lips were pursed, but with an effort, as if she had been about to speak and then had thought better of it, or had been prevented from doing so, or was accustomed to remaining silent and had not found the courage, once again, to say what she wanted to say. There was the slightest dimple on her right cheek — a quiver, perhaps, in an effort to open those lips at last, but she had restrained it. The nose was thin and delicate, almost too delicate. It made me think of noses I had seen on girls of ten or twelve, noses too big for their young, changing faces, noses grown to full size before the rest of the features had caught up, but noses towards which the rest of the character tended, like a steeple in the landscape around which the town is built. It must have made her suffer, that nose, forced her to be patient, caused her to rage, until the time came when she, her age, and her adult nose came to be one, weary with experience. And in the centre, the eyes. The upper lids all but hid the nut-brown irises; they were almost protuberant, and strangely so. They seemed to observe the progress of something hidden from me by the picture's frame, perhaps something held in her hands, perhaps something gone from her hands. Her eyebrows, the only features she had allowed to move, or maybe they had moved of their own accord because of weary surprise or unbearable sadness, shadowed her look, gave it a dappled light. Whatever this woman's eyes had seen, whatever they had taught her, had burdened her almost to the point of breaking, and the peeling paint and the creases in the canvas, the signs of ill use and age on the physical surface, reflected for me her undisclosed agony. I stared at the woman, and she stared at her invisible hands, and I followed her gaze and then stared back into her eyes.

I began to perspire, wisps of hair stuck to my forehead. The old, familiar feeling of nausea rose inside me and I felt a sharp pain under the ribs. A bell went off. A guard came up to me and explained that they were going to close. Breathing with difficulty, I hurried through the halls until I found the exit. I looked at my watch. I had been in that one room for almost two hours.

Not the next day but the day after that, I visited the painting again. It was, I realized later, a Dürer, lent by the National Library to the Louvre during repairs. There was another Dürer in the room, a larger portrait of himself at the age of twenty-something, holding a thistle in his hand. But this one single face overpowered me.

I waited till the Captain was back and we lay in bed the first night. He lay smoking his filterless Gitanes and reading a book I had already read, and I would look from time to time to see where he was, sharing the story. He opened his arms and I lay there, against his shoulder, and then I told him.

"His miraculous seeing hands. So you've made Dürer yours now," the Captain said. "He would have painted you, I think. My large, my beautiful seer."

Once, when he was fourteen or fifteen, he had been taken to Paris on a visit, and an adventurous relative had guided the boy through the labyrinth of the flea market. And there, amid the chipped crockery and the orphaned furniture, he had seen a picture unlike anything he had ever seen before. Even then, the Captain was seeking a form of perfection: at the flea market he thought he had found it, *sub specie aeternitatis*. A knight riding solemnly to his destination, balanced between the temptations of perversity and self-destruction, far from the unifying crowd. The Captain spent his holiday money on the engraving and never parted with it.

He had studied Dürer passionately, and he knew my painting well. Dürer had executed it in his fifties, at the height of his fame, probably as a study for one of his larger canvases. "He used to dream his paintings," the Captain told me, tracing my eyelids with his fingers as he spoke. "He used to wake up having had visions of great works which he could hardly remember, and jot down sketches of the visions in his diary — sketches that look like ink stains."

The Captain asked me if I wanted to return to see the painting with him. He asked this shyly, as if he suspected that it might be something I wished to keep private. I said yes. I wanted to go with him.

"I once went on a tour of museums hunting for his paintings," he said. "The Alte Pinakothek in Munich. The Prado in Madrid. The Thyssen Collection in Lugano. The Staatliche Museum in Berlin. He was one of the first European artists to see the Aztec treasures brought by Cortez to the court of Charles V. Imagine: somewhere in this face is an eye that has seen what none of the Italian artists saw. Her face is changed by the knowledge of a dying empire, and there are colours on her skin that come from gold beaten in places that did not exist in our imagination before that time."

We stood, a married couple, in front of the painting.

"Throughout his life," the Captain said softly, just for me, "Dürer collected objects that aroused his senses: snail shells, white coral, arrows made of reeds, an inkstand carved from a buffalo horn, pistachios, the skeleton of a fish. But above all he collected impressions. A bed in Brussels that could hold fifty people. The scowl of a ninety-three-year-old citizen of Antwerp. A walrus captured off the Flemish coast. A great gale at Zierikzee. His own purse-mouthed wife. And then, all the things we don't know. A cold. A flash of happiness. A flavour half forgotten. Fear. A promise. How all these inform and change the face in front of his eyes. How we change it now. The face now contains me. And you."

A group of five or six tourists had come into the room and crowded themselves in front of the painting. The older man, in shorts and a turned-down linen hat, was consulting a guidebook. The others — a couple of women, a younger man, and several children — were moving backwards and forwards as if to see better.

"Awful," one of the women said.

The younger man giggled.

"And them," the Captain added. "The poor, stony, arid minds now reflected in her face. Look! You can see her change, grow dull! Look at their sallow faces mopping up the brush strokes, pretending they understand, collectively, one man's meanings. They think they learn by submitting to taught experience, to a chorus of opinions. Cocteau once told me, pointing at a crowd that had come to see one of his films: 'Oh, be afraid of them! Their minds breed contagion!' You want to push them out of the way, drag them into the streets, away from here!''

Afterwards, in a café off the Rue de Rivoli, he shook away his anger with a laugh.

"Are my photographs reflections too, then?" I asked him.

"Are your photographs what you see?"

"What I choose to see."

"Then say so. Collect. Make declarations. Force the eye to compare. Give us memories."

I loved him intensely at that instant; I wished for large milky wings to enfold him, nurse him, thank him for not offering approval but conversation, as if saying in his deep wonderful voice that there was no permission to be granted, no doors to be unlocked, that the key to the fields was mine, and the time of day, and that the sorrowful painted face was one of an infinity of rings of which I was another, lesser sister, perhaps, but a sister, and he was grateful to be my reader. That instant I was sick with love for him, the Captain.

Not that I felt fully confident yet.

Some time later, in a small book of reproductions, I read that in Antwerp Dürer had seen the eighteen-foot-long monster of Brabo, who had once, it is said, ruled the city. I wanted to know what kind of creature it was, but found no reference to it, and never asked the Captain because I felt, in an obscure way, that an interest in a detail like this, uncalled by any larger thought, would disturb him, offend him, even, as the homeliness of the tourists had offended him, and that the pride and admiration he apparently felt for me, and for the bearing of my mourning and the discovery of my own art, and even the curious kind of honour he believed I was bestowing upon him, my husband, by visiting the painting with him, all might somehow disappear under the impression of lightheartedness or, even worse, of unintelligence, and that with that his love might too be blotted out, evaporate.

Once again he left, and once again I walked around the city, but now I returned, after almost every walk, to the room in the Louvre with my painting. I saw Ana again, and attended more rehearsals, and watched her grow more and more desperate with the play, trying to pull things together the way she wanted, and failing. She would come to me for advice. She would embarrass me by saying she admired me, envied my independence, my experience, felt helpless without me. I could never understand why.

"Nothing will come of it," she'd say about the work of all those months. "We're just jumping around and babbling stuff to one another. Why do it?"

The play had a cheerless opening. Not, as she had hoped, on the Boulevard des Italiens, but in an auditorium near the Forest of Vincennes. The two men were sick with late summer flu, and Ana and another girl tried to make up for the lack of energy. I looked for Jean-Noël but he wasn't there. I sat in the small damp theatre with a handful of other tired-looking people, watching a performance whose thread I couldn't follow. The only critic who had attended, a young man from *Le Canard Enchaîné*, left at intermission. I had brought my camera and one image sticks in my mind: Ana, wrapped in a clinging white sheet, trying to escape through the cloth, using my French phrases as pleadings, threats, screams of pain, giggles, and finally emerging, eyes downcast as in the Dürer face, her long hair curling over her shoulders, while in the back, through weak amplifiers, The Doors, I think it was, sounded a monotonous beat. I longed to tell Ana how sorry I was for her, for her failure. I said nothing: I was afraid of making my condolences sound like an accusation.

That night it rained, and I lay alone in bed, lights off, vaguely conscious of the absence inside me, to which I had grown almost accustomed, and by my side, to which I had not, and deliberately forming around me, perhaps with the intention of falling asleep, the deep burnt-umber darkness behind the face in the painting, the framing darkness out of which she rose, hair of solid gold, torso the colour of dried blood, trying to forget Ana's performance to which the long summer had led, a summer that now seemed to consist entirely of endings, of things coming to a close.

Suddenly the phone rang. I realized that I had forgotten the sound it made in my almost empty place, especially at night.

It was Ana.

At first her voice disconcerted me, as if it were disguised. There was a stilted formality to her questions, her attempt at conversation.

How was I? What was I doing?

Late-night voices have an existence of their own, detached from social conventions, from recognizable environments. They take over the speaker, fill the room, like ink spilt on blotting paper. Ana's voice usually had a laughing ring to it, a distant happiness. Not that night. There was a slurred sound that dragged itself from syllable to syllable; not drunk but difficult, as if a great effort was required to get from one thought to the next.

In broken sentences, Ana acknowledged that they had failed. The play was a disaster. Three months of work, for nothing. I kept asking if she was all right; she only spoke about the loss.

I listened.

Then Mamma died.

I used to visit her about once every four months, sometimes even less frequently. The train trip to Lyons depressed me — as did the old house reeking of mothballs, and the paint peeling off the walls, and the dark rooms that hid threadbare furniture, and the crippled maid hobbling in with the coffee. The cousins would offer their wrinkled cheeks to be kissed, and Mamma would sit in a tall bishop's chair and say nothing. In her last year I visited her once, after Easter, and then waited till after my birthday. Any holiday was a carefully planned ritual for the cousins, with ironcast rules and tacit conventions, and I felt exhausted after guarding my behaviour throughout a day-long ceremony, be it Christmas or Palm Sunday.

It was cold for November, and there was grey ice on the street, and the maid had lit a fire in the sitting-room. I had been offered a basket of knitting, which I declined. I loathed the lugubrious clicking of the needles — "Knit one for Saint Joseph, purl one for Saint Anne." One of the cousins sat in her armchair doing crochet and another was reading a novel through a magnifying glass, mumbling the words to herself as she turned the yellowed pages. They had sat Mamma up on the couch, a lace pillow at her head and a heavy woollen blanket over her lap, and Mamma's wheezing, and one cousin's mumbling and the other's whispering, and the crackling of the fire and the slapping rain, made the day seem interminable, and even the clock seemed to tick away at the one same hour that was neither morning nor afternoon. The reading cousin put the novel away and turned to a volume of pastry recipes, but she soon closed the book and recited from memory the various sweetmeats she had learned to cook in her long housebound life, and criticized, as she delivered her list, the servants' inability to prepare the *mille-feuilles*, the *diplomates*, the *madeleines enrobées de chocolat*, the *mignonnes aux cerises*. When she turned to Mamma for approval regarding the use of *noisette* flour instead of *poudre d'amandes* in the *gâteaux bretons*, the wheezing had stopped. The cousins crossed themselves, the maid was sent out in the rain for the priest and the doctor ("too late, too late for either," the maid muttered angrily), and we laid Mamma out on the couch, arms crossed, eyes closed, and a faint adolescent smile on her lips. Like an eighteenth-century plasterer executing a death mask, and much to the cousins' disapproval, I prepared my camera and took Mamma's picture. Thirteen shots, one after the other, of her face changing as if falling.

In the late spring of 1968 — in May — Ana, whom I had barely seen since her wedding, invited me to spend a week with her in the Garde, in an old farmhouse lent to her by

an aunt. It was cold and wet. As we sat in straw-stuffed
chairs she told me about Jean-Noël. First he had disappeared for weeks. Then he had reappeared one night at their
flat with a Vietnamese girl. Ana had started to scream, and
had thrown things at them (she listed the things she had
thrown, as if they held a secret meaning: the friendship
plant in the Chinese pot, the Balinese puppet, the collection
of records, the *art-nouveau* pill-box). Jean-Noël had started
hitting her. He had held her by the hair and hit her in the
face, never saying a word, while the Vietnamese girl stood
by in the dark. He had looked for places to hit her, and
carefully chosen the places on her face, her breasts, her
stomach. He had hit her for a long time. She had thought
he had broken her nose. It started bleeding, and the blood
ran down into her mouth so that she gagged. He held her
still by the hair. He kicked her legs. He never said anything.
The Vietnamese girl never said anything. Then he let her
fall into a corner. He packed his duffel-bag. He took several
things they had bought together. He also took the radio and
the jar of instant coffee. Then he called to the Vietnamese
girl and they both left.

Ana had stayed in the corner all night. The next morning
she had washed, changed the door lock and had a new key
made, and told the concierge (who had come to complain
about the noise, and stared like a sheep at her bruised face)
not to let Jean-Noël in again. But she knew he wouldn't
come back. She stuck to her promise of not taking drugs
and went through thirteen bottles of Beaujolais in four days.
A week later, she asked her aunt to lend her the house near
Nîmes. The bruises had disappeared, or at least were faint
enough for me not to notice. Her right side under her

ribcage, she said, was still sore. "Now we're both widowed," she told me. I tried to cradle her but she wouldn't let me.

"Only your Captain's coming back," she said.

It has always amazed me how the events that mark our past — our individual past, or the past of our generation or country or, if there is such a thing, the history of the world — exist outside the daily train of actions and reactions that make up our time on this earth. Days are full of waking, washing, the crunch of toast, the milky perfume of the breakfast bowls, the rustling of clothes, the fanning of money and the clink of coins, the small courtesies, lies, tiny evils, redemptions, illuminations, moments of wisdom, sleep. None of this greatly disturbs the Events with a capital E. They happen, and we continue. Afterwards, we all say we were preparing for the Event, even before, *while* it was happening, and yet there was no change of pace, no breaking of rules.

After a week we returned to Paris in Ana's battered *deux-chevaux*. Ana talked about Jean-Noël.

We entered through the Porte d'Italie, close to nine o'clock at night. Just before St-Michel, traffic was blocked. Policemen waved us to the side. The *deux-chevaux* stalled. We pushed it to the curb. Ana started to cry.

"He knew he was hitting me while he was hitting me."

A huge group coming up the street. Banners lit by the yellow streetlights, then closed into darkness under the trees, then lit again. Police in protective masks, plastic glittering. Sticks up in the air. An armoured car like a rhinoceros, headlights on. A woman in a white apron standing at the door of a *quatre-saisons* leans over and picks up a box of overripe tomatoes. In the yellow light, splashes of red cover the armoured car. Police shields go up. A torch shines, white.

"If he had at least spoken."

The group approaches, arm in arm. Explosions — the police are firing gas grenades. Under the lights, the banners read: *FORBIDDEN TO FORBID. POLICE = SS. ENOUGH OF OLD AGE. IMAGINATION TO POWER.* A grenade rips a hole in the cloth. Smoke billows up, yellow and grey. Shielded police advance, wall to wall; the gap narrows.

"The Vietnamese girl had a very small face, and pockmarks."

A loudspeaker announces that the students at the Santé Prison will not be freed. A roar from under the banners. A car parked to the right, a DS ("The goddess will serve you well"), bursts into flames. Red, orange, and blue. Sirens howl in the back but can't get past the two crowds. Heads at balconies. The students begin to rip up the cobblestones. *Aristocrats to the blade!* Somewhere, a piano.

"He never said a word but he was able to hit me."

Tear gas fired point-blank. Cries and announcements. Smells, in the following order: wood smoke, ammonia, gas fumes, petrol, burnt hair or leather, gunpowder like that of New Year's Eve rockets. A cobblestone crashes through the windowpane of a bookstore, demolishing a pile of *Essais sur les "Essais"* by Michel Butor. A bleeding woman is carried by four men, her left arm dangling to the ground. Taxi drivers are stopped on the sidestreets and forced to carry the wounded. One driver, an Algerian, stands by the open door of his car, watching and scratching his head and laughing. *My Lord, what a salad!* He is wearing a tiger-striped shirt.

"There must have been a moment when he saw himself hitting."

The blue line wriggles forward like a caterpillar, plastic shields raised. Stones repel it. It wriggles back, shouts, forward again. *Arise, the wretched of the earth.* Clutching his left eye, a man walks past us, staggering. Two old women stand at the granite door of an apartment building, arms crossed. The sirens stop suddenly, then start again. On, off, on.

"Without a word."

Throughout the night it carries on, groups dividing into groups. Here, hoisted, a bare-shouldered woman. There, hands crossed, clean-shaven, black-haired men. The police: uniforms torn, shields shattered, sticks broken. But in the police lines, no faces. The faces are in the other group, and mainly young. More than ever before in this city, I am old.

These are my snapshots. No one can say I was not there.

Nineteen-sixty-eight was the year of my fortieth birthday.

But of that May nothing remains. Barely twelve months later it had become a conversation piece. A few words were still scrawled on the wall of the Pont Henri IV, on the fountain of Saint Michael slaying the Dragon, around the Métro stop of Jussieu, but for the rest it was like an evening at the opera, a Sunday outing — "We were there." Now everyone had "been there". It was the fashionable thing to say.

The Captain came back on his last leave, and Monique threw a party for me at her house, and I realized that among those she had invited for my birthday, my ceremony of departure (or arrival), there were hardly any faces I really knew or cared about — only casual acquaintances, Monique's friends, people the Captain used to know. I had arrived (or was on the point of departing) without really having touched at many ports. Ana was not invited.

The Captain was now assigned a fixed office position at the Quai d'Orsay. All the time he had been away, the years of brief encounters and letters and missed dates, dissolved into the past.

Often, before his return, lying alone in the empty apartment, I would dream of scenes in which he and I were sitting together at a breakfast table, or planning a weekend in the country, or buying groceries or plants in the market of Rue Montorgeuil. I would act them out like puppet shows, bringing this character in, dropping that character out. We would move with stiff gestures, Punch and his loving wife, Judy, and the conversations we had had in the white-walled city of my past, and the lovemaking, everything would happen again and again between these other walls.

It wasn't like that.

I loved his shape in the morning light, sitting against the window in a rim of sunlit dust. I loved the massiveness of his form, and his old man's face. I loved the shape of his ears.

But then, during breakfast, tiny inoffensive details would irritate the scene as it took place, silently at first, then louder and louder. My nightdress would feel crumpled, would itch, would give off an acrid smell. He would look unshaven, dishevelled. The noise his jaws made as he crunched his toast, the crumb that stuck to the side of his mouth, the speck of dirt inside his nail, upset me like the sound of breaking glass. During the days of waiting I would sometimes, if I felt like it, run down and buy a baguette or a few *croissants beurre* and a copy of *Le Monde*, and then sit by that window nursing my bowl of milky coffee. Now, if I came up with the paper, he would smile at me (that was the worst part, the smile) and ask about my work (that too I loathed, because for the longest time I had nothing to show, and his curiosity pinpointed my sloth, my blankness), and take the paper from me (politely, of course) and read it silently, or break off the tips of the *croissants*, or dip the buttered baguette into his coffee so that a marbled surface of golden butter appeared inside his bowl, and breakfast would come to an end for me, the quiet and delight of the morning, and I would suddenly hate him, or perhaps not hate, but feel a surge of revulsion, of longing to be alone again, to be able to miss him, and the guilt of wishing him away, and the sadness of it all, and then the tiredness, the overpowering fatigue, and the need to begin the day by loving him.

They were brief moments, small as motes of dust, hardly worth remembering, and so easily overcome by the bliss of being together with him, my Captain, at last. Monique would ask, on our rare meetings, if all was still well, pecking at the words with a certain relish for tragedy — *Tout va bien?* — and slightly disappointed when I answered, with a laugh, that all was fabulously well. *Fabulous: legendary, incredible, absurd.* Monique didn't believe me. She thought she alone was entitled to what she called "marital bliss". Her daughters had left home by then, and the Castlekeeper had become a soccer devotee, and would sit for endless afternoons watching the games on television. This, to Monique, was a normal life, and she would have stared in incomprehension at anyone who did not envy her. Sometimes I think I did, because her happiness seemed so easy.

Ana drifted away during those months. I saw less and less of her, as if she and the Captain could not occupy the same room, the same space, but were figures in different landscapes. I missed her with reluctance, and then not at all. Two or three times her absence appeared very real — like the time when the men's urinals, *les vespasiennes*, were removed from the sidewalks of St-Germain. In the early days, Ana and I had sat at the Flore and laughed at the legs curiously visible under the iron-lacework cylinders named after the emperor who installed public toilets in Rome. We had sat and guessed at the bodies and heads that corresponded to the legs, we had invented adventures for the owners of those legs. And Ana had let her head fall onto my shoulder, shaking with laughter, and had left it there for several minutes, her hair against my face. I missed that now.

Another time was when copies of a huge book on Dürer she had once given me appeared on the stacks of remainders outside the Étienne Marcel bookstore. She had saved money, God knows from where, to buy the then expensive volume, and we had peered closely at my woman, and compared her to his images of Mater Dolorosa. And Ana had held my face in her left hand and said that I was not unlike the portrait. I took one or two pictures of myself next to that face. Of those I have no copies.

One afternoon in November, I met the Captain for lunch in the Place Dauphine, and he asked me if I would like to live for a time in South America, in Argentina. His army days were over. "After fifty you become a bureaucrat," he had said. Now there was some work to be done at the embassy in Buenos Aires, "in an advisory capacity abroad".

"For the French," he added, "the rest of the world is just Abroad."

A question of experience.

In spite of the wind we were sitting outside, watching the idlers against the façade of the Conciergerie, where once Ravaillac, the murderer of Henri IV, was imprisoned and tortured before his execution. There were leaves in the wind, and they kept falling on our table among the glasses of wine, and drawing wet marks on the green plastic top.

"I'm not fond of all this," the Captain said suddenly, waving a hand at the strolling men and women, at the wet wind, at the bony branches. "The buildings, the streets, the weather, the trees — I feel as if we were walking through a derelict room full of junk, leftovers, discarded history. And I the only survivor. And you," he added, reaching over to hold my hand.

"I will miss Paris," I said.

"Truthfully," he answered, "I don't think I have ever missed anything."

I kept the coaster from that lunch inside Montherlant's *Les Filles* and then, when I lent Ana the book, inside one of my boxes of photographs.

Among the dead.

We made arrangements to leave after Christmas, when the streets were clogged with filthy snow and the buses were full of people coughing and angry and unwashed. And I looked at it all, loving it in spite of itself, because I imagined I had been happy here.

I called Ana one last time, and we met at the Café de Flore "for memory's sake", but this time we sat inside. The tables and chairs on the sidewalk had been pent up for winter behind thick glass partitions, and we went into the *salle* and settled down on the wine-red plastic seats, and ordered hot lemon grogs that steamed in glasses held tight by metal skeletons.

We didn't promise to write, we knew we couldn't promise to visit one another, we didn't give each other advice, but when we said goodbye Ana threw herself into my arms and slid her hands around my waist, and as I held her tight, feeling her small, hard body against mine, I realized almost with longing how she could use her nimble body to make herself attractive, to ask for protection, and I wondered why anyone would want to harm it, how anyone could do anything to it except cradle it, enfold it, rock it to sleep.

I watched her walk away, under the yellow light of a corner bookstore, and then cross the street without looking back and blend into the moving crowd.

BUENOS AIRES

WHERE IS Buenos Aires?

Years later, in my Argentinian house, when I was empty-ing my boxes of photographs onto the floor, preparing them for destruction, I found the Paris coaster again, hidden between the images of another time, little windows all since walled up. Faces, bodies, snippets of landscapes, tops of armchairs, doorframes, street perspectives, couples embracing, solitary sitters, groups in funny poses. Some have zigzag edges, others have no edges at all.

Buenos Aires turned out to be a patchwork of my other two cities, a mongrel Algiers in which the grimy arcades metamorphosed themselves into baroque French palaces, and the vast flat houses gathered around a cool courtyard hidden behind Napoleonic façades from the fifteenth district in Paris. Crowds like my African crowds sat in sidewalk cafés like Parisian cafés, and men with copper faces pushed past me in suits from the Avenue Matignon. The traffic and the apartment houses were Paris; the trees and the music in the suburbs were Algiers. I would sometimes stop at a corner, bewildered, transported to another corner left behind long ago. Many times I felt homesick.

The photos.

The brown smiling face of a fat woman with straight short black hair. (In photographs everyone smiles. I let them.) Her dress is flowered. Behind her is the grilled door of our house in the district of Belgrano. You can't see the huge moulded walls, the long windows with iron shutters, the balconies, never used, behind which lay the bedrooms hidden by long gauze curtains and satin drapes. Her name is Lorenza; she cooked, she washed and ironed, she loved posing for the camera. She also served dinner when we had embassy guests over, or the new business acquaintances of the Captain, and then Lorenza's young cousin came to help, Rebecca, a girl of twelve or thirteen who was quite good in the kitchen.

Lorenza saved all her money (she slept in a room on the back terrace) and sent it to her husband in jail. Every Sunday she visited him. The bus ride was almost two hours there and two back. She was fifty but looked ageless, too old to be an adolescent, too smooth-skinned to be old. She had come to Buenos Aires from La Rioja during the fifties, when Perón called to the poor "to come and seize their fortunes". Like so many others, she took this to mean Buenos Aires, "the heart of the nation", "Babylon on the River Plate". She slept in a house made of corrugated iron behind a wall rimmed with broken glass carefully embedded in the cement. Later she moved to her uncle's house on a quiet tree-lined street, a house with a big courtyard and dusty grape vines. She had worked as a cook at a German lady's, and when the lady had died, her daughter had recommended her to someone at the French consulate. She had learned to cook dishes whose names she couldn't pronounce. She loved my couscous, and compared it to the *locro* they prepared in her province. While she ironed, on Thursday afternoons, listening to the soaps on the radio, I watched her and felt hopelessly useless. I decided to do what I had not done in Paris: keep a record, this time for myself. For the first time I used colour film. My first portrait in colour is of Lorenza against a red wall, her skin almost fading into the red.

Another photograph, blurred:

Florida Street, the shopping district, before they cluttered it with flowerpots. Among the throng of hurried faces, office clerks, messenger boys, women frowning, and tired old men, a middle-aged woman in a blue suit trimmed with white, blonde hair, a blue purse at her side; the arm from which it hangs appears as crooked as a teapot handle. The photo is out of focus: I have to peer closely at it to make out the woman's contours or her expression, and when I do, I see that she is screwing up her eyes just as I'm doing now. She is Angélica Iturralbi, the writer, author of a dozen novels, many of them published not only here in Argentina but also — as she is fond of pointing out — in Spain. Mrs. Iturralbi is a bestseller. Three American students have written theses about her work. *The Meat Merchants* and *My Name Is Esperanza* were made into films, and her collection *Stories for Afternoon Tea* was adapted for television. She writes a weekly column on women's issues in *La Nación*'s Sunday magazine. We met because she wanted to interview me as the wife of "someone" on the French embassy's staff.

"We Argentinians have always looked up to France, more

than England. Fashion, literature, architecture, food — all the important things come to us from France," she wrote to me. Would I see her at her apartment for a drink one afternoon, at six?

Mrs. Iturralbi's apartment (she had divorced twice, both times in Mexico, because in Argentina divorce was still illegal, but she had kept her first husband's name) was furnished in the style she called "our Louis XV": ornate gilded frames around huge mirrors, inlaid tables with ivory and mother-of-pearl, curved-legged chairs with padded backs and Chinese birds stitched into the fabric of all the upholstery. The drink was scotch. Mrs. Iturralbi (I never called her anything but Mrs. Iturralbi, even after we became friends) spoke excellent French — a little formal though, a little old-fashioned — and asked me what I thought of her "vast vaporous country". I had been in Argentina only a few months, I barely knew the change of seasons, I hadn't learned the language. Mrs. Iturralbi answered for me. "This country would be extraordinary if the inhabitants were not so lazy."

"No one works, *really* works; no one sets an example. In the years before the wars, the European wars, my father was an ordinary man, but rich by any standards." Her father, not herself: Mrs. Iturralbi insisted she was in her early middle age. "The peso was worth two dollars; now. . . ." She lifted her glass and waved her free arm dramatically, as if to embrace the unknown.

She had tried to chronicle "the descent into hell" from demagogue to demagogue, from corruption to corruption, in her novels. Had I read them? Only one, alas, had been translated into French. *¡Trabaje, Hombre, Trabaje!* had become *Le chant du laboureur,* published in paperback.

"Not a very nice edition, but we can't be choosers. I received a congratulatory letter from Escarpit, and of course nothing but silence from my colleagues." She pressed the book into my hands. And I would have to read her column, which would introduce me to "the real Argentina". Last week — had I seen it? — she had written about the lack of attention given to the upkeep of the city's public parks. And the week before, she had written about the growth of the slums, which, she maintained, had begun during Perón's first dictatorship. (She loathed the ageing dictator; he had forced her father to sell his houses and apartments and live a life of quiet misery. She saw Perón in brash neon colours, a plexiglass demon.) "The writer is the country's social eyes, nose, ears," she said. She felt it was her obligation to bear witness. "This miserable task," she said, "has become my gospel." She rang for the maid to bring some more ice and offered to refill my glass.

There are photos of other encounters. With the Rosales, an engineer and his wife who befriended us early on; with Mirta Beckstein, the owner of the gallery where I finally showed my pictures; with the French ambassador. My own favourite showed Mrs. Iturralbi next to a copy of one of her books, with her photograph on the cover. The two faces — both in black and white, one framed by the edges of the book, the other by the margins of the photo-sensitive paper — question each other.

Another: in front of a smoking brick barbecue stand two men in open white shirts. One is the Captain, smiling, looking embarrassed. The arm over the Captain's shoulders belongs to a black-haired, moustached man. The hand dangling from the arm holds a spatula. A unique feature of this photograph is that the moustached man isn't smiling. His face is wrinkled as if in a smile, his cheeks dimpled, his forehead lined, but his eyes have an angry look, an anger that seems heightened by the Captain's presence. His name is Colonel Casares and he shared an office with the Captain.

"Casares doesn't think," the Captain would say to me. "He acts on a large and meaningless notion of duty. He knows that there are things he must do, and that he must do them because they are his duty. And when asked what his duty is, he will tell you that duty is the things he must do." Casares' wife was a thin, dark woman from the north. He had once caught her reading a book of poems by the Communist poet Neruda and had set fire to her entire small bookcase. She would tell this anecdote as something intensely funny, gasping for breath as she laughed her way through it. They had four children, three boys and a girl. When we went to their country place on a Saturday or Sunday, I'd watch them play, and notice how fast they grew, and wonder whether my dead one would have looked like the boys or the girl. I sometimes envied Mrs. Casares.

March 1972. It had been another hot summer. (My life is a succession of identical seasons, from summer to summer, from the dry air of Algiers to the humid air of Paris, from the humid air of Paris to the dank air of Buenos Aires — civilizations without air-conditioning.) A barbecue at Colonel Casares' place in the country. Trees, a duck pond, a swimming-pool, a huge bougainvillea sprouting from the arched walls of the house, purple on pink. I walked about this half-wilderness, barked at by two German shepherds. In the middle of an alley of eucalyptus I stopped. Framed by the memory of Our Lady, I made promises about what would happen If, what I'd do When, If Only, Please. There was nothing I wanted to happen, except this. *Let it not be lost*, I prayed. *Mother of God, grant me Your indulgence.*

What frightened me most was the shadow of the other, the dead one whom I had not even named — unsexed, unshaped, unborn. Now my dreams were about entering empty rooms, silently, or walking down corridors towards closed doors that magically swung open in my presence. I kept telling myself that arrival occurs after departure, let it be, let it be. I felt that if I had given the other a name, it would be easier now.

I had a name for my new baby.

Thought became more difficult, less strict. I could not concentrate. I stopped dreaming. My sleep was filled with webs of colour, no forms, no voices. The inside of me possessed me fully, and I allowed myself to sink into that feeling — a self-acquiescent haunting. When I told the Captain, once again his face lit up with joy.

Photos of myself, once a month until the birth. A growing sequence which I framed and hung along the wall beside the staircase to the second floor. One month, two months, three months. I stopped before the birth itself, November 15. *Feasts of Saint Albert the Great, bishop and doctor, of saints Gurias, Samonas, and Abibus, martyrs, of Saint Desiderius of Cahors, bishop, of Saint Malo, bishop, of saints Fintan of Rheinau and Leopold of Austria.* No girls.

There are no photos of the actual birth; all I remember is the pain. And then, through gritty eyes, the extraordinary prune-coloured face with insect arms and legs grasping and kicking. The first thing I did when she was brought to me, caterpillar daughter, was seek out her crumpled fist and open it, like prodding the lips of a closed flower — the fingers, the tiny fingers, brittle fingers, and face creased inside sleep. The Captain held her to his own face, then laid her down in the cradle of his arm, his hand a concave pillow.

That was the first photograph of my Ana.

I wrote to Ana in Paris that I had given the baby her name, and sent her the picture. I watched my Ana sleep, eat at my breast, watched her watch the moving world as if she could follow the movement of the sun and all the stars. In the dark silence, at three or four in the morning, as I held myself to her lips while the Captain slept (sometimes he'd put a companionable hand on my thigh without even opening his eyes), I would compose long explanations about the world for her, so that she would not stumble or have to grope or guess, and sing her the Algerian songs I had once heard on the other side of the Earth.

Two days after Ana's birth, Perón returned to Argentina.

He had been in the country almost a month when the Rosales asked me to tea at their house, in one of the green rich suburbs of the city. As the rented car turned into their street, it was stopped by a sudden crowd. I asked the driver to let me out and, clutching Ana in one arm and my paper-wrapped offering of *petits-fours* in the other, I pushed my way through the people and opened the gate to the Rosales' house. Alberto Rosales was there to meet me.

"They come to gawk," he said. "To catch a glimpse of his eminence, of the king himself. He has taken the house just down the road, but he will find it far less regal than his palace in Spain."

"We call it the Return of the Mummy," said Laura, guiding me towards her red velvet couch. "It's been like that for weeks. I've absolutely forbidden the servants to go near them."

"The servants are all peronistas," said Verónica, the Rosales' thirteen-year-old daughter. "They have a right to go."

I asked if he ever appeared.

"Of course he does. Twice a day, with those disgusting little dogs of his. Round about this time he takes them for a walk."

I put Ana on Laura's lap and pulled my camera out of my bag.

"I won't be a minute."

I ran outside and made my way through the crowd. The house they were watching was a whitewashed affair guarded by a single policeman. As I looked on, the door opened. The crowd cheered. For a moment nothing happened. Then, slowly, it appeared, the oval face we knew so well from the blue and white posters, a face creased and yet polished, as if the lines on it had been drawn in pencil on an egg, the black hair sleeked back, the mouth cut in as if with a knife, the Roman lips, the arched nose. He lifted both arms in a gesture he had made classic and spoke a few words of thanks and greeting, as if welcoming his public to his stage; then, while his henchmen were warding off the journalists, he started walking down the street pulled by the dogs. My picture looks like a collage: on one side, the single, isolated houseowner walking his pets, a private and unextraordinary event; on the other, the journalists and fans, kept away by big-shouldered men — old combatants from the Party, young militants from the guerrilla groups — and bothered neighbours whose retreat had been invaded by the savages. The public life.

The Captain hardly spoke of his work here: any references to it were uttered in a bored and boring tone, as if he were looking towards an end very soon in sight. He was now in his mid-fifties: he seemed to have reached a fullness of age, grown into his features, as it were, and it was hard to imagine that soon he would retire — the French army packed its men away at sixty — and be part of the generation that sits on park benches feeding pigeons or playing chess. He spent most of his time at home with Ana, talking to her as if she could understand his words, and I know I felt jealous, especially in the evenings, until the baby was asleep and he would talk to me again.

Occasionally he'd discuss politics.

"I sit and listen to them," he would say. "I listen to the generals arguing about how best to use Perón and his comeback. I listen to them string long words together like amulets they hang around one another's necks. They are convinced of having missions, for the most part. They are like saints in search of painless martyrdoms, and believe in effortless duties and rewards earned by good intentions. They believe they can bring in Perón and his court and make magic."

Once, walking down Cabildo Avenue under the jacaranda

trees, looking into the shop windows that seemed to replace daily the solemn and dignified elephantine houses that reminded me of El Biar, we were stopped by a man in a dark suit, smiling under a thin moustache.

The Captain introduced us: the man, also a captain, kissed my hand and spoke admiringly of the weather.

"The country's back in harness, I would say." He smiled. "Just a few more stallions to turn into geldings, and we can sleep peacefully at night. Our Perón hasn't lost the touch, has he?"

The Captain nodded and was about to say goodbye and move on, but the other put out his hand and held him by the arm.

"And let me tell you something from the heart: we're all grateful to you, to France, for not letting us down in our hour of need. Evita, God rest her soul, would have shaken your hand."

"I met her once," the Captain said.

"And?" The man lifted one hand as if weighing the Captain's admiration.

"She seemed to know exactly what she wanted," the Captain answered.

"A magnificent woman. She had balls," the man added. "You will excuse me, *señora*, but she deserved to be a man. Isabel can't touch her, can she?" And he laughed to show he knew the Captain agreed with him.

"*Allonsenfan!*" he sang out, and walked on.

Sometimes we wondered whether we would make our home in this strange land. We imagined Ana growing up in the soft sung Spanish of the country, learning in years to come the moral fables of her grade-one readers blurred by the bureaucratic realities of everyday living — what Mrs.

Iturralbi called "a *Doppelgänger* existence", saying one thing with ironic petulance, and acting another unashamed.

We settled down to a comfortable routine: walks on Sunday morning down the avenues of closed stores, a film once a week in the neighbourhood theatres, meals in restaurants almost every other day because we enjoyed the late-night bustle of Buenos Aires, where nothing ever seems to disrupt the eating and drinking and flocking into the streets, badly lit because of the energy cuts.

We made love seldom: sometimes on Sunday afternoons, in the large cool bedroom with shutters like those in Monique's house in Algiers, but less out of lust than out of companionship, and less out of that than out of sadness. In Buenos Aires one becomes prone to melancholia.

One Sunday the Captain was called out early in the morning. When he came back after midday — I was feeding Ana in the kitchen — he told me that Perón had died. The French ambassador had been notified and he and the Captain had been called to Perón's house in Vicente López.

For two days the body lay in state inside the Building of Congress. Perón had requested that, unlike that of Evita, his body should not be embalmed. The face that surfaced from the folds of clothing was a hairless, desiccated animal, crouching, eyes closed, in a corner of the coffin. The Captain obtained for me special permission to photograph the dead man, and the image I chose looked concave, as if the face had already fallen to dust and only the space it occupied remained for a moment hung in mid-air.

I shook hands with Isabel Perón, swathed in black, weeping hysterically behind her veil. She was now the President of Argentina. "Courage," a small man in a pinstripe suit kept saying behind her shoulder. "Courage." And each "courage" seemed to drive her again into a paroxysm of tears.

I drew back and rearranged my camera, but the small man came up to me and said, very softly, almost pleading: "Don't, please don't take any more pictures here now. The dead general, well, God hold him in His infinite grace, is beyond our influence; but here we need to preserve all the energy we can. Understand? So kind. Film seeps up the spiritual strength, you know that. And Isabelita needs all the strength she has right now. Poor angel."

Laura Rosales had accompanied me to the Congress but had stayed by the door. As we walked away, she said: "That was López Rega speaking to you. The man who consults the oracles. Pigeon's liver, tea leaves, that sort of thing." And then, with a sigh: "As long as this doesn't mean more chaos. We are so tired of chaos! I don't know how much longer we can take it."

When she repeated this to the Captain at a café table, the Captain eased his hand over the folds of the white tablecloth: "Ironing out the creases is what you are talking about. How much would you be willing to give up for peace and quiet? What sacrifices would you make, Laura?"

Photographs make you believe the past is fixed, like prints to paper, glossed over with a polished sheet of metal. That faces don't change, that places remain the same. I love (I

am aware of using the present tense) the Captain's face in
these photographs.

Once Laura Rosales asked me if I believed the stories of
people being rounded up and taken away and tortured.
A neighbour had come to tell her that her daughter and
grandchildren had been "taken away" by police in civilian
clothes. Rosales himself had told her that the woman
watched too many thrillers and that one had to be careful
what one believed.

I answered that, like photographs, reality lends itself to
many interpretations.

Early one morning, I found Lorenza comforting Rebecca in
the kitchen. I had come down to get Ana's breakfast ready
and sit with her at the table before she set off for playschool,
and for a moment didn't notice that there was anyone else
in the room. Lorenza was sitting in a corner, holding her
cousin's hand. She wouldn't tell me what had happened,
saying only, "a disgrace, *señora*, a disgrace".

"I told them politics were bad," she said. "We are a good
family, *señora*. Never had anything to do with politicians."
Rebecca was sobbing.

Later, after I had spoken to the Captain about Rebecca,
he seemed extraordinarily troubled. Then he told me that
from what he could gather a brother or brother-in-law of the
girl had been found dead in one of the garbage dumps. He
agreed that it would be best for her to stay with us, at least
for a while.

The dead body decomposing into garbage, chameleon
patches of clothing, cardboard, skin, hair, vegetable peel-

ings, rose behind me, already a memory. I asked the Captain if he thought the government was responsible.

"People are responsible for their own deaths," he said.

Rebecca shared Lorenza's bedroom and helped with the housework. That morning her crying had embarrassed me, as if I had caught sight of her undressed, but it was the only time I saw her cry. Afterwards her presence in the house became expected.

One day, as I was sorting out my photographs on the dining-room table, she stopped sweeping and said she also had some pictures.

From her pocket she pulled a grimy snapshot, in black and white, of a young man in a soldier's uniform.

"Jorge," she said. "My brother. During his military service."

She put the photo down among mine, which were large and in colour.

"They told me what happened. A man put a bag over Jorge's head. He made Jorge kneel down. He put a pail of water in front of Jorge. He pushed Jorge's head inside the water. He let Jorge pull back, then he pushed Jorge's head in again. The man did this several times. The last time Jorge drowned."

I looked at the photograph and then at her, and I took her in my arms, and burst into tears, and told her how sorry I was. But she pushed me back, gently, and said that it was all right.

"Not your fault, not to worry, *señora*."

She let out a small laugh and told me that Jorge had not

chosen to do his military service in the navy because he couldn't swim.

"He was afraid of drowning, *señora*."

A photo from the series I showed at Mirta Beckstein's gallery:

Plaza de Mayo, the Government House gleaming pink in the distance, over a sea of white-kerchiefed heads, women asking the government for their missing children. In the foreground, blurred, one single face, a featureless Eumenide.

Another photo: grey peeling arches, like the arcades of Algiers. Same brindled wall, like a cow's hide, same brown wrinkled soldier's face, like a walnut shell, perched at a grimy table. On whose side is he?

"This war has no uniforms," as Mrs. Iturralbi was fond of saying.

Another: children in white school pinafores — Indian faces, Scandinavian faces — and behind them a huge teacher, a nightmarish version of themselves. The Captain says that in the provinces the schools lack everything — pencils, books, heating. This photo was taken at Olmedo, fifty kilometres from Buenos Aires, near the country place of Colonel Casares.

Another: lilac-spotted trees and brick-dust paths, and a huge bronze lion snarling towards an invisible prey. I used to wheel Ana through the park of Palermo, through the old willows and jacarandas and ceibos. Verónica, the Rosales' daughter, sometimes came with me on days when school was out. Sometimes she would offer to take Ana on her own.

Sometimes Lorenza would come and replace me while the Captain and I met for before-lunch drinks at one of the cafés next to the Recoleta Cemetery.

From Palermo you could walk to the Recoleta, and from there, past rubber trees as large as Norman towers, you would reach the French embassy, where, from time to time, we attended an official reception or a party.

Christmas of '75 or '76. The French ambassador's wife has decided to have a *bal costumé*. I know the heat was appalling, in spite of the electric fans, but the dates become blurred here; the memory of the events themselves is clear, but the grid of months and years has shifted.

The French ambassador's wife is a crane. Her dress is made entirely of white sequins and feathers. Her face is a long black beak. The ambassador is a turkey. Layers of grey feathers surround his chest and stomach and a gelatinous red substance droops from his crown and chin. Colonel Casares — I recognize his voice behind his bearskin — is saying: "Let's not fall into a sin of pride; we're not infallible in our judgements. When we act in a political capacity, we continue to be Catholics, just as priests continue to be Catholic when they act as civilians."

The turkey assents: "A state of siege. Wise measure. One thing is certain: you are bringing some order into this madness."

The bear: "Christian order, Your Excellency."

The crane: "And we all appreciate it."

A horse gallops into the room and collides with a waiter, causing him to upset his tray full of glasses of champagne.

The horse shrieks and rears its front legs. A parrot jumps onto the scattered glass and does a tap dance on the shards. The powdered glass glistens.

The horse turns towards me and the Captain: we are both in Tuareg dress, hidden behind veils.

"Congratulations," says the head of the horse.

"A wonderful party," says the Captain.

"I think we have cause to celebrate. A death, a birth, the new millennium, what?" And both back and front giggle violently.

A lion and a tiger stand under a Christmas tree twenty feet high. Little white birds and crystal balls decorate the branches and a Neapolitan angel blows his trumpet at the very peak. Under the boughs the French ambassador's wife has set up a nativity scene, exquisitely carved (so she says) in Bahía in the early nineteenth century. The lion holds up the Infant Jesus and says that Christmas has always seemed to him a political celebration.

The tiger: "Indeed, indeed."

The lion, holding up the figure of Jesus: "I wonder if Perón copied the raised-arms gesture from Him. *Pax vobiscum!*"

The tiger: "Bishop Witte told the seminarists that they were reading Christ's doctrine too literally. Christ spoke of the poor, but he meant the poor in spirit. He did not mean the poor poor. In Argentina the poor in spirit are the rich."

Daphne turning into a laurel tree stands in a distant corner. I approach her with bacon-wrapped prunes stuck on toothpicks, one in either hand.

"The Italian industrialist they kidnapped was found hands tied, shot through the head, in a slum. He was sitting on a wooden crate and the whole room was covered in newspapers. Even the windows were papered over with *Crónica* and *La Razón*. There was a TV set in the room, and nothing else. The bastards got their money and then killed him. Not one of them older than twenty-five, they say. Merry Christmas."

"But they caught them?"

"Oh yes, they caught them. A trial is too good for them, but we live in a democracy, unfortunately."

A shaggy dog: "Woof, woof. I'll lift my leg against your tree."

Daphne (letting out a scream): "Martín, stop it! Stop it!"

"I'm the spirit of our national literature," says a voice next to me.

I turn round and see a collage of books, costumed dolls, photographs, and other bits and pieces. I recognize Mrs. Iturralbi's voice.

"These are characters from my latest novel; and this guitar is *Martín Fierro*. And this page from an encyclopedia represents Borges."

Mementoes: we are given small beautiful gifts. I receive a pearl brooch in a silver setting; the Captain a glass paperweight which the ambassador says once belonged to Chateaubriand. (I am furious at the thought that the objects whose existence depends on ours outlive us and remain immutable, uncaring, pristine. I once would have thrown the brooch into the North Atlantic, were it not for the knowledge that by returning the pearls to the sea I would have been granting them a firmer immortality.)

The turkey makes an announcement: "Ladies and gentlemen, my dear friends. I want to thank you all for being here, I want to thank you all for allowing me to be here, a stranger in a strange land. You welcomed me, as you have always welcomed France, and France has not forgotten that less than two hundred years ago the provinces of the Río de la Plata followed our Revolution. France is, in a way, the Mother of all Republics, and I've made a pledge to offer you my country's assistance in preserving yours. *Joyeux Noël!*"

A duck waddles in and announces dinner.

It was Mrs. Iturralbi who insisted that I have an exhibition of my work. A friend of hers, Mirta Beckstein, had bought a small gallery on Florida Street and was not reluctant to show photography as well as painting. I asked the Captain to help me choose which ones to hang.

He seemed excited as a child. We spread the contents of my boxes over the living-room floor and throughout one whole night, after he had put Ana to bed, we looked at picture after picture. He said he had not realized how much I had achieved, how hard I had worked, how strong and clear my images were. He said I had found a style, a voice, an eye.

I suddenly felt ashamed of things I hadn't told him, like the half-eaten sea monster. There among the photos strewn on the floor, I wanted to stop and tell him. I didn't.

The exhibition opened without much fuss. The wife of the French ambassador came (unofficially, of course), and Mrs. Iturralbi, who had written an over-affectionate article in *La Nación* which had, in turn, attracted a group of *femmes savantes*.

A young bearded man, his camera ostentatiously dangling

from his neck, asked me if I was the "artist", and when I said yes, complimented me on my work.

"You'd hardly notice they were taken here, in Argentina, today," he said. "What European ability! What understatement!"

I asked him what he meant.

"Understatement? There's a photo by a German photographer, taken at Buchenwald or some such place. There's a huge pile of bones, human bones, presumably. And just at the edge of the pile there's a dog pulling at one of the bones. You see, the dog doesn't know they're human bones. All the dog sees is food. And he's right, of course. A dead body is also food."

"My work is mainly portraits. And yes, indeed, it's what I choose to see."

"Ah! Choose! How nice to be able to do that! I did a series of portraits once. Only you couldn't see the sitters. Just the blank wall behind them. *Desaparecidos*, you see? No understatement there. I'm sorry, I didn't mean to be rude."

I asked him if he was working here, in Buenos Aires. He said he was, and maybe one day I'd come and see his work.

I said I would.

That night, helping Mirta close up at the gallery, I asked the Captain if he thought my photographs hid something; if he thought I was being hypocritical or blind, or both.

"Because you are not making statements?"

"I think I mean that, yes."

"I believe you make choices," he said. "To work the camera you make choices. To find a frame you make choices."

"What if I make the wrong ones? Choose for the wrong reasons? Pretend something isn't there?"

"My dear," he said, "the reasons don't matter. The results matter, the thing we see when you have finished. No one will ever know why Dürer chose to paint that one face you are so attracted to. No one will know why you chose this" (he pointed at one photograph) "or this" (another) "or this" (a third).

There are books I associate with certain foods, certain places, but most of all certain smells — the Balzac spiced with thyme from our kitchen, the Dante reeking of smoked wood, Papa's *Tartarin* and the smell of his tobacco, Jean Rhys and strawberry jam on toasted baguettes in the Paris sun. Some moments of lovemaking are like that: attached like lichen to a certain tree. The night of my exhibition we made love quietly (it had been weeks, and now Ana lay asleep in her bed next door), for a long time, happily, stifling laughter from pure enjoyment, and the house was full of the smell of photographic chemicals which the Captain said reminded him of the military laboratories during the early days of his career. And I said to myself that I was also making love to his words, and to the thought behind his words, and to the experiences of years and places that lay behind that thought, years of stone and dust and green cut grass, and seasons, and all the books he had read, the music he had listened to, the paintings he had seen, and I remembered, again and again, that he also had made choices, had made one choice, had weighed and measured and considered, and in the end had chosen me.

The Captain was looking forward to his retirement. Sometimes he thought of returning to the Normandy of his childhood; other times he wondered whether it would not be best to choose another place, a place "less trampled by History" (as he put it), and he described to me the coast of the Gaspé in Quebec, reaching into the Gulf of the St. Lawrence, about which he had read many years ago. "A land of seagulls," he said. "No more bureaucracy, no more beating experience into rules." A few times he had been sent by the embassy to other Argentinian cities to help out with matters concerning France — the establishment of French companies, research needed prior to investments, banalities of diplomacy. Once he was sent to Rosario, where piles of neglected documents had been discovered at the French consulate. The honorary consul, a jam manufacturer who had been appointed to the post as a favour to the governor, had allowed visa requests and import permits to collect unattended over almost a year, and the French ambassador had — so he said — received too many complaints. "I'm France's messenger boy," he would moan.

Above all, the Captain loathed leaving Ana. He had grown accustomed to their morning play, watching her learn with the detachment of a cat, laughing at her tricks. He seemed constantly amazed at the transformations in her, and yet he knew she had begun to change the very first time he had held her, minutes after her birth, and had become, through invisible conjuring, a chubby two-year-old, an inquisitive four-year-old, a quick, graceful five-, six-year-old drifting further and further away from him into forests of her own.

"Who will love her when she has grown?" he said to me,

as he held her one afternoon when she had fallen and grazed her elbow. "Who will take her away, change her name, sleep with her? Whom will she love?"

One winter morning, as I returned from taking Ana to the kindergarten around the corner, Lorenza came to tell me that Laura Rosales was here. She seemed very disturbed. She couldn't find Verónica. The evening before, Verónica had left for one of her extra-curricular university courses as usual — her first year studying law — and hadn't returned. Laura had lain awake waiting for her (she could never fall asleep before hearing the click of the front door and Verónica's soft tread on the stairs, the bathroom light going off, and finally Verónica's bedroom door shutting in the dark) and about six in the morning had asked her husband to go and enquire at the house of one of Verónica's friends; the phones, as always, were out of order. She herself had tried a number of places — the professor's apartment, the university, her sister's house in Caballito — with no results. Her husband had done the round of hospitals. So many young people seemed to be getting in trouble these days; but Verónica was different. Laura was going to the police. Would I please come with her?

The Central Police Headquarters in Buenos Aires has the air of an Italian *palazzo* seen through distorting lenses. It squats in the centre of the older part of town, too large on the sides and sunken on the top, stained with age and crumbling. Long queues of people waiting for papers (documents are issued here) serpent their way around it, and from rickety booths police guards with machine guns survey the doors.

The first guard sent us to a window where, after some delay, a small old man with round glasses asked to see our identity cards. He stamped a piece of paper, handed it over with shaking pulse, and sent us up the palatial stairs, which smelt of urine and disinfectant. On the second floor the landing divided into countless corridors, each pierced by doors, and outside each door sat small crowds of people, waiting. Women in white pinafores moved in and out of these doors carrying fat cream-coloured folders. We stopped one of the women and showed her the paper. She pointed to a door at the end.

We waited standing among the small group outside. A dark-skinned woman with large eyebrows tapped on the paper and said, rather than asked: "Your son, your daughter." "My daughter," Laura said. "Me too," the woman nodded.

Almost an hour later the group had not yet moved and Laura was looking ill. I stepped forward and knocked on the door.

A tall woman opened it.

"What is it?"

"We've been waiting for an hour. We've come. . . ."

She didn't let me finish.

"Wait your turn."

She was about to close the door, but I held it open with my hand.

"We don't even know who we're supposed to see. It doesn't say on the paper."

"We don't give names. Will you move, lady?"

"Please be quiet," the dark-skinned woman behind us whispered.

I kept my hand against the door.

"I just want to know who we're seeing. This woman is looking for her daughter."

"Everyone's looking for a daughter, a son, a husband. . . ."

I pushed.

She let go of the door and yelled to someone inside:

"Sánchez, these people are forcing their way in!"

A young policeman appeared behind her, machine gun in hand.

"Let's go," he ordered.

"What's happening?" asked a voice inside the office.

"Nothing, inspector," the policeman answered. "A couple of troublemakers."

The door opened wider. The inspector looked hot and uncomfortable. He wiped his moustache with the back of his hand.

"Who are these women?"

"This one with the funny accent was trying to get in," said the woman, pointing at me.

"It's about my daughter, she's missing," Laura pleaded.

"All these people are looking for someone gone missing," said the inspector. "This is a police station, not the pound. You people should keep your relatives on a leash." Then, turning to me: "You're French? I can tell by your r's."

"Madame Berence!"

From a distance someone called my name. Colonel Casares.

"What are you doing here?" he said.

Suddenly everything changed. Introductions were made,

the inspector apologized, we all shook hands, and, to the tall woman's intense anger, we were shown into the room.

The inspector listened to Laura's account, shifted through a pile of papers, and pulled out a long typewritten list.

"This," he said, "is the list of those reported missing yesterday. Yesterday, you understand? One day, that's all. Then they all come back, it turns out they had a drink too many, stayed with friends, decided to seek their fortune because Mummy and Daddy were being too strict. You can't be too strict, can you?"

"Verónica is not like that. She would have called, left a note."

"No one is like that. That's what everyone says. Every son, every daughter, is a saint. Mrs. Rosales, those are the ones the agitators get hold of, they are tempted . . . with politics, drugs. . . . Look, I'm not trying to frighten you, but you should have kept a firmer eye on your daughter. She'll come back, you can be sure of that, tail between her legs. Remember the prodigal son?"

With that the inspector showed us to the door.

Colonel Casares accompanied us downstairs.

"Don't worry, she'll be fine. And we'll do what we can to find her. But you heard what the inspector said. She's bound to come back, ashamed and feeling silly. Don't be too hard on her then. Youth!"

A few blocks away we stopped at a café. Laura looked haggard. I suggested I'd speak to the Captain that night; maybe he'd know someone we could ask. We sat in front of the small coffee-cups of thick white china, and it occurred to me that I could calendar my life with these stained white circles, full stops that kept my score in each of the cities I had lived in. Laura lit a cigarette and inhaled deeply. Then her fingers rolled the tip of the cigarette against the edge of the ashtray, back and forth. I put my hand on her wrist.

"Laura. . . ."

"Excuse me."

The dark-skinned woman who had sat outside the inspector's door was standing next to us. In the light of the café window her face appeared curiously spotted. Her very wide eyebrows gave her a comical look.

"May I sit down?"

Without waiting for an answer she pulled out a chair.

"I heard you in there. They never do anything. They put you on file, then. . . . Who knows? Maybe they just throw the files away."

The waiter appeared and she ordered a coffee.

"My name is Marta. Marta Corrales. I'm a widow. My daughter disappeared six months ago. With her husband. And her children. You want to see their picture?"

From her handbag, black and creased like a mammoth prune, she pulled out a snapshot of her family. The young couple were standing behind their three children. The smallest — I couldn't tell if it was a boy or a girl — was wearing a Superman T-shirt. The woman recited their names, pointing at each of her grandchildren with a witch's finger.

I asked her what had happened to them.

Neighbours had told her that men in civilian clothes had broken into her daughter's house one morning before dawn. No one had actually seen anything, but they had heard doors slam and a car pull away, tires screeching. The house looked ransacked. The police put down in their report that the house had been vandalized "by persons unknown".

"And then?"

"Nothing happened. No one would give me answers. Finally I met another woman who was looking for her children too. A boy and a girl. She took me to meet other women. They too were trying to find their children. There are so many, so many."

Laura looked up. "Verónica is not like that. She's never been interested in politics. She's a child. Verónica is a child."

Mrs. Corrales stood up again. She hadn't touched her coffee.

"Why don't you come and meet the women? Maybe we can give you clues, suggest ways."

I put some money on the table, under the tin plate with the bill.

"I think you should," I said to her. "There doesn't seem to be anything else to do."

The women met in a large, almost unfurnished apartment on Bolívar Street, in a district of large rooming-houses and old cafés. The room we sat in, on wooden benches, had a metal desk and a filing cabinet, and on the walls framed with ornate mouldings were charts, a map of the city, and photographs of the missing.

Mrs. Corrales introduced us. There were ten or twelve women in the room, most of them our age; a few were younger. One or two looked older than they probably were:

they were sitting at the desk, sifting through papers. One by one, they spoke.

"My daughter disappeared while we were on holidays in Mar del Plata. She had gone to the movies with some friends. They said two men pulled up in a car and dragged her away screaming. I've never heard from her since."

"My daughter was pregnant when she disappeared. They came to our house, said they were from the police, took her away. Later, at the station, they told us they had never sent anyone, and that we were maligning the good name of the police force."

"My husband was in the metal-workers' union. He was arrested during a union meeting but the police deny having any record of him. Another member of the union told me he had heard from someone else that my husband had been taken to Azul."

"My son and my husband disappeared one morning going to work. They are doctors at the Ramos Mejía Hospital. Some time ago they treated a man brought in by the police with serious burns. The police told them the man had fallen over a bucket of acid. My husband insisted on filing a report. They warned him against it. The man died that same evening."

"My grandchildren, a boy and a girl, were taken with their parents to prison. The police told the neighbours the children would be brought back. I've been able to speak to my daughter at the Women's Detention Centre, but she has not had any news about the children. Nor of her husband. One of the guards told her she should be wearing widow's weeds."

"My husband is a teacher at the Buenos Aires National High School. He was stopped by three or four men one afternoon after class. The students told me that the men forced my husband into a car and drove away. They threw his books into the street; the students collected them and brought them over to me. I haven't heard from him since — almost a year ago."

Suddenly one of the younger women stood up.

"I can't take it any more!" she screamed. "Tell her what happened to me! Tell her! Tell her about Toti, about Alfredo, about Carmen, about Mrs. Epstein, about Andrés, about Sonia, about Carlos, about La Negra! Tell how we saw them, heard about them, read their letters, read what others had seen! Tell her about the rapes, the beatings, the torn-out nails, the broken bones, the electric prod, the suffocations. . . ." She caught her breath. No one moved.

"My daughter, Paula, was taken in. They made her watch as they tortured her husband, Néstor. I repeat their names every time I can — Paula, Néstor — because we know they never say them. They tell you your children don't have names. They tell you your children don't exist, that they have vanished. They want to force you to miscarry your sons and your daughters, to believe they were never born alive, to think of them as bloodstains on a carpet, as unfortunate accidents. The word they use to insult them is *"aborto"*, abortion. They call your children abortions, they make your children unborn. Néstor, Paula. I can't. I can't take it any more."

One of the older women came up to us and pointed at the filing cabinet.

"You are welcome to look through those files. They contain hundreds of declarations. Some from those who escaped and went into hiding. Some from those who escaped and then were killed. Some from those still inside, smuggled out God knows how."

The younger woman was bent over, retching.

Another woman stood up:

"What I don't understand is how it can be done. How you can actually hold a live human being in your hands and deliberately cause that being pain. I mean, deliberately choose an instrument to cut it, to bruise it, to burn it, to deliberately set your mind to think of methods that will harm it, guide your thoughts into the flesh. I mean, if you have held another person, another extraordinary hand with its beautiful fingers, or a head, if you have ever held a head against your shoulder, with the hair and the eyes and the tongue, how can you then deliberately cause it to bleed? How can you hurt it? How?"

Laura put her hand to her mouth as if she was about to vomit. I helped her up, and in the bathroom splashed water on her face.

"Don't wait till tonight. Ask the Captain now if there is nothing he can do to help find her. Please," she said. "Please."

Mrs. Corrales offered to accompany Laura back home and I hailed a taxi to take me to the Captain's office.

The building in which he worked stood alone among vacant lots where other, similar buildings had once stood but, less fortunate or protected than this one, had been demolished in the early seventies. It had two fronts: a main one, looking towards the city, towards the grey Algerian arches of the Paseo Colón, and another, hidden, looking over the brown river that spread into the distance towards the Uruguayan coast. Outside the main door a group of small children were playing.

My mother and your mother
were hanging out clothes.
My mother punched your mother
right in the nose.
What colour was the blood?

I had never come to this building before. For the first few months the Captain had worked in an office on Santa Fe, overlooking the Plaza San Martín, a beautiful *fin-de-siècle* palace now occupied mainly by the Argentine military, who had set aside a wing for the use of the French embassy. I had gone to see him there a few times, but I disliked the official courtesies, the voices that changed according to who you were or who you were married to. Then, after the trip to Rosario, he had been asked to help with other bureaucratic tangles in another military precinct. "This new place is dreadful," he had told me before moving there. "It's like an abandoned university building, full of empty cubbyhole offices and derelict lecture rooms."

A grenadier directed me to the enquiry desk, and a creaky elevator with folding grilled doors took me up to the tenth floor. All the lower floors up to the seventh had wooden planks nailed over the openings.

The elevator stopped short of the landing, and I had to climb out over a high step. Grey corridors ran in four separate directions, and there were no signs indicating the office numbers. Long flickering neon tubes lit the ceiling but the bottom half of the walls and the entire length of the floor were in darkness. My foot kicked an empty tin; an old newspaper fluttered in the warm air. The place reeked of mould and unwashed linen. I started walking down the first corridor to my right and soon came upon a row of numbered doors.

The office number the man at the desk had given me was 1038. On the frosted glass of the first door I made out "1012". Then 1008, 1056, 1024. There seemed to be no sense to the order in which the numbers appeared. The corridor divided into two, and I turned again to the right — 1030, 1002, 1096. Then, at the end of another turning, 1038. I tried the door but it seemed locked. I tried the next door along the corridor, 1044. It opened.

I was at the top of a lecture theatre. The ninth and tenth floors had been combined, at least in this wing, to make room for several tiers of seats. There were some fifty men in attendance, their hair cropped short in the military fashion. Below, in the centre of the theatre, was a small table and a blackboard behind it. The Captain stood between the blackboard and the table.

It took me a few seconds to recognize him because I had never seen him from above, and he looked shorter and older. Then he lifted his eyes, but didn't see me. He was talking to the men on the tiers.

In his left hand, pressed against the table, he held what looked like a celery stalk. In his right hand he held a knife. For one long vertiginous moment I imagined that he was going to lecture on cooking. "He knows nothing of cooking," I thought, absurdly. "What will he teach these men?"

The Captain was speaking.

". . . a task in which detachment is absolutely essential. It is you, you yourselves, that you need to watch above all, watch with the attention of a cat. I understand that skaters need to forget all sense of normal walking at the moment of skating; their balance depends on it. The innate sense that propels one foot in front of the other will creep in when the skater is trying not to plod but to push, not to raise his foot but to slide it. You must forget that you too can walk. The skates must be extensions of yourselves, parts of your body. At this moment you have never been walkers; you were born skaters.

"Your patient, on the other hand, is only a walker. He (I say 'he' but of course it can be, and often is, a woman) has brought his condition upon himself. Your patient is responsible for the situation that has been created, is guilty of the situation, has in fact surrendered every right which you, as skaters, have. What you must tell yourselves is that the patient, not you, is the contractor; that you, not the patient, have been called in to serve, and that you must carry out your task with unflinching care. Your personal feelings, your fears, your philosophical musings, are of no consequence in this matter, and must, like the sense of walking, be left aside. Above all, you must remain decent men after your task is over.

"Every task has an objective. You may be told that certain information, a name, or place, or date, must be obtained at all costs. That is not, must not be, your concern. That is the task of the interrogator — or, to continue my image, the judge at the skating tournament. Your business is not to draw conclusions from the performance but to sustain the performance.

"Of what does this performance consist? It consists of an elaborate and extended act of destruction. You, who are men with a certain familiarity with death in combat. . . . Or perhaps not, as your country has not taken part in a war since the last century. And yet, you do know that death is not destruction but cancellation. It puts a stop to the present, but there is nothing death can do about the past. It is like setting a limit on the number of houses to be built on a certain site. No more houses will rise after the moment of death, but the ones that rose before will stand there and bear witness. Therefore your task is even more far-reaching than the task of death. Your impossible task is to erase the past.

"Pain can destroy. Pain is, in fact, so powerful that the very idea of pain can destroy. The knowledge of pain in others can destroy (this is, once again, the thing to guard yourselves against). Even the expectation of pain in others can destroy.

"What I have here, this piece of vegetable life, is essentially identical to your patients. It has skin, it has flesh, and its inner leaves can be seen to correspond to internal organs and bones. The only important, very important, difference is that it will not react. It will not scream, plead, cry, or clam up. To that aspect of our task I will come later.

"When the knife approaches the skin the destruction begins. It begins before the knife actually touches the skin. The knife establishes the nature of the ensuing relationship: metal and flesh, linked. The first insertion" (here he lowered the knife and gently let the blade partly slice the outer stalk) "provokes surprise. Surprise from the first pain, surprise from the alien presence, the blade, inside the body, and above all, surprise because the pain is less than the patient expects it to be. To this surprise, and in spite of the pain, is joined a shameful sense of relief.

"The second step affirms the destruction. Relief may lead

the patient to suppose that the process may, or even will, be reversed. You must make certain that there is no doubt that what is taking place is for ever. You draw away the knife" (he did this with uttermost care) "and, holding between your fingers the detached end of the strip of skin, you pull outwards and away." (In his right hand he held a torn vegetable ribbon, the green filaments hanging down towards his palm.)

"Now the flesh is open to the air. Now the patient knows that the procedure is one of absence, that he will never recover the loss. And all the time you must tell yourself: I am not part of this foreign country, this alien body, this other suffering. It is he, the patient, who has brought this on himself. I am but a labourer. I am doing my job. And I must do it well.

"You will find it important to remember this in instances when one of the water methods is used. Your job is then to make the patient relinquish land for water. Holding the patient's head down, you will be returning the head — not the patient's entire body, only the head, a creature unto itself — to the water. It is, if you will, an act of repatriation, a change in the weather. If death occurs, it is always due to the patient's stubbornness, like that of someone unwilling to dress warmly in a snowstorm. 'To drown' must not, in your vocabulary, be a transitive verb. You must repeat to yourself: no one ever drowns. People choose to stop living. Drowning is a suspension of the will."

I backed out through the door, turned along the corridor, down the ten flights of steps, into the street, back home. I sat in the bedroom, and I could hear Lorenza calling, and Ana crying, and later the Captain saying my name, and still I wouldn't open the door, and then as the night wore on and he came in at last, and tried to touch me, and then left me, and as I turned to the wall and tried to sleep and suddenly felt hungry and thirsty, and as I remembered that I hadn't eaten, and as I told myself it didn't matter, the fiercest pity and sorrow and nausea swept over me like darkness, and I said to myself, *I can't love Him*, I said to myself, *This is Another; this is not Him; this can not be Him*, I said to myself, *I love Him still; I can't understand how, but I love Him still.*

And in that country, and in the next, and in the changes of season and climate, in the house we left and in the one we came to, in the vast anonymous Argentina behind and in the vast anonymous Quebec before us, in the land that bleaches all sins, becoming, like the land, something without a past, I realized that I would go on loving him in spite of my eyes and my ears, in spite of myself, and all I could do to rid myself of the question was to turn to fire, to consumption and ashes, which I myself would carry like the madwoman of Lorraine. And then I could understand what was meant by it all. It meant that something was finished.

The road from Anneliese Michault's house to ours isn't long, and the afternoon is cool in spite of the sun. I told Anneliese I would be fine, and I will be fine, and she likes to see me step out of my cocoon, walk in the world again, come out of hiding, unprotected by Rebecca. During those last days in Buenos Aires Rebecca tried to tell me that she thought she knew, that she thought I knew. *"I can look Señor Berence in the face,"* she would say, not certain that I understood.

"I can see him move and talk and be with you and with Ana. How can I believe?" And then something changed.

I never said a word, I never told her. But I heard her and the men talking of explosives. *Fire to fire*, I thought, *but when?* And then at last she led me to Anneliese's, and took Ana by the hand, and said to Ana in her comic voice, *"Play with Matthieu till the evening."* So it will be now, this afternoon, as he and I lie together in the darkened bedroom, and sleep will come like an old unbroken habit, and we shall burst into flames.

And in the darkness, the fluttering and the whispering and the rustling sounds around me will gnaw their passageways deep inside me, making my skin rise in mounds like burrows, inhabiting me like the ghosts of small furry animals that breed and fight and tear up flesh in my throat, bloating me, stifling my voice, as they did that first night when I knew, and all the next day, and the next, and the next, until today, until now, because at last, at long, long last, I no longer expect the sorrow of waking up in the morning.

HERE

A̲NA SAT by his side waiting for him to speak, because
he had always comforted her. She sat with the seatbelt done
up tightly around her waist, feeling more trapped than
secure, sick with sadness, and all at once so immensely
tired that she knew she must not allow her eyes to close or
she would drift into sleep, and there she would be alone.
She saw his hands crouched on the steering wheel, his eyes
turned forward towards the onrushing road. She waited.

Then he spoke.

Is the door properly shut, is the seatbelt fastened, sit back,
listen, there's so much I want to explain, now your mother's
dead, your poor mother's dead, come to an end, the end she
sought out for herself, brave to the last, we all have to learn
how to finish, because death is not important, did you know,
even her death, my death, even your death, my Ana, my
daughter, because everything runs its course, and the

choices are yours, and she decided to stop, and we go on, and you must decide how you wish to go on, and therefore listen, because I need you to understand, because I will give you a choice, and you can't choose without understanding, before we reach Quebec City, oh certainly, long before we reach Quebec City, and ask me questions if there's anything I say that sounds difficult, that needs clarification, because even though you are my daughter, and I your father, I am also a man who has lived through many odd and different years without you, and only at the end do we come together, you and I, only in these last long specks of time that seem so full and fast to you, changing so rapidly, no time to think of how they are changing, what it is they are changing, no time to look at yourself minutes ago and see yourself turning, so fast, into something else, the strange creature that rises behind your eyes as it did just now, fierce or frightened, something I can almost grasp every time I look at you, as if you appeared to me behind sheets of running water, and at times I can almost make out your features but at others I can only remember you as I think you are, as I think you were, and I'm certain you've thought the same thought once, that if the face we have changes, and the way we look changes, and I don't mean only growing, I mean learning, and wasting, then which of those faces are we, which of that string of faces like the faces of a dead person throughout the long night of a wake, waxing and waning, as in one of my first memories, when I was three or maybe four, in the big house at Étretat, in Normandy, with windows drawn away from the coast so like the coast here in the Gaspé, the long black drapes on the door and the mirrors turned, because Mère Félisie had died, Mère Félisie, my father's mother, your great-grandmother, whose eyes are now yours,

and in the dining-room, a long dark dining-room where the
silver glimmered and the furniture smelt of apples, on the
dining-room table they had laid her coffin, and I was lifted
up by one of my uncles to see her face for the last time, and
he held me there as I looked at the butter-coloured cheeks
framed in lace, the thin lips, the closed eyes, and as I
looked, all that long, long moment during which my uncle
held me, as I was watching, Mère Félisie's face began to
change, it grew grey and then flushed and then seemed to
slowly fall as if the bones inside the head held it no longer,
and I screamed, and the uncle put me down and told me I
was a coward, and I didn't think about it for the longest
time, and then it came back, many years later, when I was
trying to make out how my own face had changed, in front
of my shaving-mirror, and how the world had changed with
my face, and maybe the same thing happens to you, maybe
something you've forgotten suddenly springs up, like a book
you've mislaid that suddenly falls from its shelf, like the
Jules Verne book you lost and then you found and drew in,
when I became so cross, because you did not keep it as a
book, as I do with my books, but as a shell or a corpse, and
then there it is, and nothing can truly explain where it was
all that time, if it was really there, hiding, secret beings,
books, "my visitors", you once called them, maybe because
you felt there were those things your imagination held and
others it only received, guests from elsewhere, requesting
lodgings, some for the night, others for long uninterrupted
periods, still others, the rarest, demanding lifetime resi-
dences with acres and acres of land through which to wan-
der, forbidden acquaintances, I thought when I was your
age, dangerous strangers, perhaps because they were not
always there, perhaps because at home your grandmother

believed that books had a faintly scandalous air about them, that they were beyond her control, that inside their cases, bound in leather, they hid strange music, invisible pranks, because the china, the cut glass, the varnished furniture you could see motionless in their seclusion, but words, stories, flowed through black scribbles that could not be grasped until explored, the sin committed, so there were few books in the house in Étretat, and they were lined up like old people on a thick oak shelf, less important than the Sèvres china, a Bible, *The Golden Legend*, two or three books by Chateaubriand, Renan's *Life of Christ*, and a gazetteer in whose two-columned pages I first saw the places where later I lived, as if one's sight could then skim forwards as well as backwards, look and see, ah yes, in this place I'll be happy, here I'll despair, there I'll die, instead of the wearisome trying out, trying out of place after place, time after time, so much useless wandering, and where does it begin, because it always seems that beginnings lead to understanding, accumulations of cause and effect, like the changing air outside the car and the greyness in the failing light beyond and a hint of rain, the trees still green scratching the surface of the storm clouds and then the first few drops, that's something I can remember, a walled garden and a lace netting to protect from insects or cats, and then quietly, the net filling with dark spaces, clouding over, and something wet and cold landing on my skin, wonderful rain, ah, surfacing memories, how closely I was watched by the neighbours, a boy correct in velvet and silk, the son of the late Monsieur le Docteur whose fingers had prodded the most intimate and invisible parts of their bodies, whose voice had dictated their bowel movements and eating habits, hours in bed and walks in the afternoons, the son of the late

Monsieur le Docteur had to show exquisite manners, had to be humble in his memory, had to be supervised for fear of setting bad examples, my readings, the objects I looked on, the friends I played with in the gravel back garden of the house in Étretat, chosen friends like the son of your grandmother's cousin, "The poor dear is so keen on you," your grandmother used to say in an indifferent voice I loathed, "you must set an example for cousin Bernard," his pale mop of hair stuck to his forehead, so unlovely, "Go play with cousin Bernard, go walk with cousin Bernard, show cousin Bernard the old dock on the beach but be careful, watch out where it's slippery," and cousin Bernard would of course fall into the seaweed water, or step into it on purpose, his fishy smell even stronger now, and of course I would be blamed, "You pushed him, Antoine, your wickedness is beyond endurance," and then the deprivation of supper, double prayers, and the apologies, until the next time, again and again, until one day I said no, my first No, a beginning or end, I can't remember your first No, my Ana, your first choice, you yourself taking shape, coming together like metal filings around a magnet, but my first No I remember exactly, because we had gone out together, cousin Bernard and I, another of those excursions carried out year after year, to visit our old or sick relatives, Madame Enriquez Berence, Aunt Dora, Père Boniface, especially Père Boniface, the minute, wrinkled priest of Notre Dame de Grace, who on Holy Thursdays would bless the sea and command it to respect the limits set by its Creator, Père Boniface, the only one of all your grandmother's relations whom I did not mind visiting, in spite of the acrid smell of his low-ceilinged presbytery, the smoky heat from the always-lit fire, the library full of green leatherbound books in low bookshelves surrounded by convoluted black furniture — I remember the griffin claws clutching the wooden apples that served as supports for the legs of the chairs, and in one of these chairs Père Boniface sat, toes barely brushing the carpet between the griffin claws, asking trivial, uninteresting questions, and cousin Bernard would reply politely, and I would reply politely, and then Père Boniface would say, "You must be hungry, my children, let me see what I can find," and disappear into a dark kitchen with its whiffs of orange scent, and reappear with a silver pot of chocolate and a plate of thin and egg-yellow ladyfingers which your grandmother had told me not to accept the first time offered, but wait politely till the second time, and then take only one, and thank him for it nicely, and not dip it in the chocolate, and cousin Bernard took two, and sat there, mop against his forehead, until Père Boniface went back into the kitchen, and then, quick as fire, cousin Bernard stood up and ran to the bookshelves, pulled out two or three books, opened them, tore out a handful of pages at random, ripped them out of the books as if he were ripping out the hair of a doll he hated, threw the pages into the fire, and returned the books to the shelves, and sat down again, peering at me from under his mop gleefully, defiantly, as Père Boniface came back to offer more chocolate and ladyfingers, and I was incapable of saying a word, I felt sick at the thought of Père Boniface the next day or the next year taking down one of his beloved books, opening it at a passage he knew almost by heart, and finding the pages torn, the few words hanging onto the jagged end of a wound, and not understanding, not knowing who or how, incapable of guessing, while cousin Bernard, alone in his room at night, would smile, cousin Bernard would imagine and enjoy the thought of the old man standing where he had stood, surrounded by griffin claws, perhaps weeping, and I thought, I never want to know how this is done, I never want to be able to follow cousin Bernard from the idea to the action, from the thought of tearing the book or causing pain to the old man to its realization, I never want to be cousin Bernard, I want all my deeds to have a reason, so now I can talk to you under the warm rain, as the car breaks curtain after curtain of water, as the running patterns collide with the windshield and are swept away by the wipers, as they come at us faster and faster, and grow as they come, and vanish, as the whole world turns from colour to colourlessness, from forms to a smudged page, a washed-out slate, a beginning, once again, for me to try and help you understand that there, that one time, I did not approve of wickedness, I found it so repulsive, so revolting, that I said I would not see cousin Bernard again, and accepted being locked up in my room day after day, no dessert on the tray brought by the tearful maid, Fabiola, with her one bad leg, beautiful thin leg that made her hobble up and down the stairs and corridors, made her move as to a dance, until they gave up and the excursions with cousin Bernard were no longer mentioned, and I knew that I had won something, I had achieved something I hadn't known was there, like landing upon an undiscovered island and taking possession of it in your very own name, and then came other summers, and time spent looking through old books that showed rotogravures of the Great Works of Mankind, horribly detailed pictures of the Conquest of the Alhambra, the Expedition to the Source of the Nile, the First Locomotive, people with prophetic faces looking towards sunsets or sunrises, discoverers like myself, until one day, in a small history book, I think it was, there I saw Masaccio's

Christ laid out upon the stone, yellow and dead, feet first, gnarled, wise feet, and I wondered that dabs of paint could make me see this, that swirls of the brush, scrapings, shadings, could put such overwhelming beauty on a piece of dead canvas, and I thought, I am making this, the painter is dead and I am turning this into live matter, without me this marvel would not live, and later in the library at the Lycée in Tours I found Ruskin in Proust's translation, and Proust, not Ruskin, told me how to lie in the grass in summer, or in the dark dining-room, and fall into a book, into Jules Verne, into Karl May, and, again, make it my own, my own adventures of Captain Hatteras, my own millions of La Bégum, my own raft down the Orinoco and my own treasure in the Silver Lake, have you not felt that, my Ana, the sense of infinite possession, your eyes and nose and ears like exploratory armies conquering the world for you, laying it at your feet, yours, Ana, to do with as you please, dependent on your wish, you, giver of life and breath, and to find among the booty one perfect jewel, which for me, later on, was my Dürer in a Paris market, discovering that I, Antoine Berence, had caused it to be in a manner in which it had never been before, rescued it from dust and destruction, and one evening in the Tours cathedral, the music of Telemann slowly rising around me, like drops of wet sand building towers by the water, my hand dropping the notes in secret corners of the mind, and no one knew, and there was no one to tell, and for others it would disappear, be gone, but not for me, carrying the invisible treasures around the Lycée, the Lycée with its big draughty halls and huge oak doors and a yellow tiled courtyard in the middle with a fountain where we would congregate to talk, and then President Doumer was murdered, and the teachers came to class wearing black armbands, and in the chapel the priest told us that God had extended his hand over France to make us atone for our sins, because every one of the drops of blood that fell on the pavement when the president died had been caused to fall by our hands, each and every one of us, and I thought then, he doesn't know what he's saying, he is talking of a God Who will make things for destruction, he is talking of Someone Who would not care, doesn't care, and not Someone in Whose hand I sit, he doesn't understand that, on the contrary, He loves us for our sins, as I loved Fabiola when she stood by the sink in Étretat, her black skirt pulled above the back of her knees, her thin leg so much more exciting than the rest of her body, white like the unicorn's horn I later saw at the Museum of Cluny, ebony white, until one day she turned and discovered me, and grinned, and crossed her arms and grabbed the hem of her dress and asked me if I had ever seen a woman naked, and I was filled with the wildest fear, and I ran and hid myself in my room, and I wondered then, as my body grew and changed, and my voice broke and my skin became sick, what sin was mine for the giving, guessing at hideous acts in sepia-coloured magazines strewn over the barber's table on the expeditions led by my father for the ritual haircuts, the cologne-scented room, the floor littered with tufts of hair, the smell of tobacco and onions mingling with the haircreams and shaving soaps, while the men talked of politics and town gossip, and I felt prudish and shy as an intruder, knowing myself condemned, alone in the entire world, guilty of a filthy act, followed through the night by the finger of God, which smelt like the barber's finger as he held back my ear for the blade, asking myself, high on the barber's chair, for what blemish would I be loved, what secret was my covenant and in what light did God see me, as He saw the radiant beauty of the Buffus toad, or looked into the drawn and wrinkled snout of a Java bat, loved the slug, the sea-cucumber, the spiny and leprous stonefish in its coral bed beneath the sea, and I began looking for those dark lights in others, a glimmer here, a glance there, but soon I realized that these, being of God, are unintelligible, appear uninteresting, banal, that Mephistopheles is a fiction and no one swirls his moustaches in public, and that I was to tend my own walled garden within, nurse the minute yellow tentacles deep inside the layers after layers of a rose, and that the layers made the core invisible, the invisible eye of the rose, and that prepared me, I think, for when we all stepped out into the streets, the Lycée behind us at last, as the old Blum government collapsed around us and we began the war, tried on uniforms, listened to orders, and started to grow accustomed to the coarse rasping of voices, cloth, skin on our hands, the sights, the long streams of men and women and children walking one after another along mud roads, dead horses in ditches, trees stripped of their bark, and the house in Étretat blown to rubble by our own men because of a mistake, the frenzy of chance, and sitting in a ditch, caked in mud, trying not to notice the lice slowly crawling down the marshes of my body, and I thought, this is when those secret sins will flare up, watch for a flicker like a lit match, the sergeant cutting himself a larger ration, the soldier leaving behind his friend with the gaping wound, the army priest too terrified to deliver extreme unction, but then I thought, no, these are not secret at all, these are simply festering, waiting to be executed one day like the three classic impossible things, and then, after the Germans leapt the Maginot Line where cousin Bernard died, it was summer, and everyone was waiting for something to happen, a mixture of dread and exhilaration, and in Paris the water of the Seine had gone down and green weeds had collected all around the rims of the quais, and the stench of the mud rose into the streets, and there in the shops and in the cafés and in the restaurants, wherever you looked, there were no anti-Germans, no one was an anti-invader, anti-Pétain, anti-anything, because there were no victors, victory cannot be attained, victory is not within the reach of mortals, mortality snatches victory away from us and all illusion of eternity is a hideous joke, and the people sat as usual drinking wine at the round marble-top tables, playing *pétanque* in the brick-dust squares, walking in pairs across the bridges, and yes, there were armoured cars and troops, and German flags with the spider cross flying from the tops of the department stores, but if there were voices against them, they were mumbles, and if a few people threw stones, they were no more frightening than children throwing pebbles, awkward, morose children, like the children who marched out one morning, cold it was because winter had come early, led by a tall thin man without an overcoat towards open trucks waiting at the tip of the Île St-Louis, where the first saint of France, who was also a king, read out the benediction to his subjects, and the people who had come onto the balconies to feed the last sparrows or shake their eiderdowns in the chilled air, or simply to look down on the city old with mist, called out to the man, "You, the Pied Piper, why are the children following you?" and he looked up and told them that the children were following him because they trusted him, and the people thought the yellow stars sewn on the children's coats looked comical, and they called down at the children, "So small and with such a big star," and a few of the children smiled because they had been taught to smile at the jokes of adults, and the people went back into their houses slamming their blinds and windows and lowering their sashes, and the trucks were loaded and pulled off, and then it felt a little warmer, and the morning was allowed to begin in earnest, and I thought, now perhaps I have seen it, letting everything simply happen, like poor Pontius Pilate, because nothing holds the core together, nothing speaks to all and every person, because Paris is as Babel, and the woman at the newspaper kiosk spoke Greek, and the waiter Italian, and the gentleman reading Cicero in the restaurant English, and we spoke French, and the soldiers German, and everyone went about his business, and I went in and out of streets with other soldiers, and in and out of bars and schools and houses, and nothing changed, and here they would serve a German colonel, and there they would ask to see papers, and one heard rumours of troops moving here or troops moving there, of people rounded up in the night, of So-and-so the baker or So-and-so the teacher being led away, but no one was ever heard to say anything except a grumpy "Ah no!" or a gruff "I'm fed up!" or, at most, a kick at the chair and a curse as if they'd lost at cards, or upset a glass of brandy, or burnt their hand on a lit cigarette, and afterwards they said they didn't know, they hadn't heard, they never guessed, except that some remembered having seen the long trains, the departures, having heard, as in a dream, the breaking of doors at night, the shrieks in the Marais courtyards, they had suspected, been reluctant to believe, and so when all was cleared, and the dead counted and the survivors sent home, and the generals' hands shaken and the razed houses rebuilt, and new trees planted and new streets named after new freedom fighters, new treaties signed, fifty-five million lives lost, and I began to wonder, where is the knot that binds all this together, the balance between colours in a death by Masaccio or a portrait by Dürer, the notes that sound as one in time, layer of memory after layer of memory, the map traced by a book, by the progress of the story and the progress of the characters and the advancement of ideas and the proliferation of images, all that which points to an order, an order without which the colours and sounds and words will disperse, without that order my blood will splash against the receding walls, my bones will shatter, my nerves will burst in tangled webs and cling to the wreck of this one supreme explosion, and so I must try to find that centre, that last intimate and perfect point which I must try to reach and hold still, on a path marked with incidents, so difficult to explain, as if you could make a history of your life in so many chapters, moments you remember as you change, moments sticking like flies to flypaper for no known reason, a teacher at the Lycée standing in front of us all, reading Racine, tears streaming down his cheeks, or the sister of Jean-Marie, best friend, perhaps, sitting in her father's armchair, skirt pulled up above the knees, underwear the colour of her skin, or the discovery of *Les Caves du Vatican*, the knowledge that a deed could be committed for no thought, no reason, and the fear that my reasons were excuses, or the afternoon I saw a very young couple being pushed into a car by an even younger German soldier, and the couple was laughing, and the German soldier turned to his superior and said, "Why are they doing this?" — *they*, he said, not *we* — and the day I turned thirty I looked again at my face in the mirror and didn't recognize it, because I was supposed to have the face I had had at fifteen still there

under the layers of stubble and sagging skin, and I accepted
my age, and so it was that in 1955, I, a captain, followed
twenty thousand other soldiers to Algeria, the only one, I
imagined, to carry in his knapsack *Le Trésor de la Poésie
Française*, whose compiler, Monsieur Bertrand Lavech de
Valério, had announced on the cover, "No Living Authors
Included", a book of which Monsieur Clive made fun often,
a book that through the days kept me awake with thoughts,
like Évariste Parny's "Distrust the white folk, you denizens
of the coast," Lautréamont's "Old ocean, great bachelor,"
Hugo's "The heart spread wide through countless wounds,"
Ronsard's "Matter remains and the form is lost," and in the
bone-white city of Algiers, which you, Ana, haven't seen,
in the small bright streets and houses black inside, the lines
kept coming back with other meanings, that distrust was
bred from those who undermined the law, that the sea was
everlasting and constant, that the flesh destroyed counted
less than the heart, and that the matter did remain in the
end, because I loathed, because I have always loathed
violence, because it makes me feel sick with a nausea
greater than anything else I have ever felt, when once, near
the steps covered in human excrement that lead down to
the sea in Algiers, I saw the gulls sweep over a cat trapped
in a gap between the stones, a yellow cat, a very thin yellow
cat, a very small, very thin yellow cat, and the gulls swept
over and down and measured the reach of its claws, and
screeched as they let themselves fall and be carried away,
but in doing so pecked at the cat, only to eat the eyes, and
the sweep was so sudden, so fast, so light that you could
not see them do it all, they just flew down and flew up, and
the blinding simply happened, one moment there was a
clawing cat and screeching gulls, and the next the cat was

screaming as I had never heard anything scream before, and its bloody eyes were all that told you something had happened, pure violence, unnecessary, resulting in nothing, serving no purpose and therefore lacking passion, and nothing can be built without passion, maintained without passion, passion at the service of order, but I never told your mother what I had seen, I didn't know how to tell her, I would have wanted to, I know, I would have wanted to hear her reasoning, I loved to learn from her thoughts, her passion, so different from mine, able as she was to wring her passion into shapes she loved, and what I most feared, the treason of attachments, never frightened her, she gave into them gladly, and every night when she came to bed, her face washed and the scent of her brushed teeth upon the pillow, clean as stones in a river, I loved her for it all, and my silence never seemed a betrayal because it was guided by my love for her passion, a passion like the one that guides and protects the law, as Sergeant-Major Grolier used to say, a sergeant-major who had taken his vows in the Benedictine order and had preferred to serve God through the army, and I remember his face very clearly, it was long, drawn out, as if his features were tired, and he suffered horribly in the sun, and he was in charge of explaining the new country to us, the strategies, the pitfalls, because we had all had lessons in geography, history, anthropology, in France, but we all knew we needed the memory of those who had lived through it, and Sergeant-Major Grolier had lived through it many times, the assassination of the young couple of French schoolteachers, liberal-minded, full of good intentions, or the bus full of children outside Oran, or the bomb in the Milk Bar where he had seen, nestled in the cup of a tree, the hand of a fifteen-year-old girl ripped off her wrist by the impact, and again and again he repeated, we are not here to punish, we are here to stop, because the carnage has to stop, and because it has to stop we will win, and to win we must know, and to know we must ask, and he had devised a method of getting at the answers, a method of going painfully back through the branches of the Algerian guerrilla, because if A had chosen B and C as his allies, and C had chosen D and E, and E had chosen F and G, to return from Z to A he needed at least as many steps as A had needed to reach Z, and that meant bringing in one by one every member of the underground, every member with no exceptions, every man and every woman, and every child if necessary, and our task was to learn to ask properly, as when looking at a painting, seeing that segment in connection to this other one, seeing a colour touched by those beyond it, or look, just like the rain keeps draping the windshield, the triangle that comes back, again and again, a window on the world, oh so fleeting, gaps of the heart, Sergeant-Major Grolier used to call them, find the gaps of the heart, and so many of us never understood it, Clive among them, poor fool, his need for friendship making him believe we were comrades on a mission in small desert towns, boy scouts talking about the world and its course in the heavens, and he simply fell behind, Monsieur Clive, whom you so dislike, a mangy horse trying to carry the day's workload from sunrise to sunset, inefficient, well-meaning, lonesome Monsieur Clive, embarrassing me with the memory of a now unintelligible companionship, because we grow, we are purified, and I and three or four others at most, nervous as at a first-year exam, and the sergeant-major had the prisoner brought in, the patient, as he called him, always say the patient, and the patient stood in front of us, a thin small man with a black moustache, as frightened as we were, and the sergeant-major ordered him to undress, proceed, he had told us, as if you know all the answers, as if you know all the questions, as if you are only doing this for the patient's benefit, the patient undressing, a folding cot made out of stuff that looked like cheesecloth, flimsy as a spider's web, a small desk, a chair, two pails of water, a portable telephone, and a flickering gas lamp, and the patient waited, trousers still on, and the sergeant-major yelled, "Quick!" because the Arabs are very shy, their naked bodies are never exposed, private to themselves and God, and the sergeant-major stood up and that was enough, there the patient stood, like a small child wearing a moustachioed mask, and then we started the questions, easy at first, then louder, until the sergeant-major thumped a fist on the desk and ordered the pails of water to be poured on the patient, and then took up the prod, which I had failed to notice, and tested it in the air, and spoke to us slowly, no longer asking questions, explaining how the instrument worked, how the electricity coursed through the prod and over the wet body, because water helps the pain to spread and prevents the skin from burning, it is up to us to find ways to make use of the pain, pain is a greater challenge to our imagination than pleasure, and above the patient's whimpers and howls, like the whimpers and howls of an animal, the sergeant-major explained that one must not rush the prod, one must take one's time, one must pause for the questions to be repeated and for the body to recover its strength, so that the pain after relief will seem increased, and the mind dreads the relief as much as the pain, and he explained all this quietly, telling us, when you speak, be gentle now, the yelling is over, the patient will shout but you must remain calm, imagine you are the dentist, say to the patient, "Just a little more, just a touch over here, let's see what we can do, this is going to hurt only a moment, be brave, be strong," because the patient must trust you, in the end he must turn to you for guidance, in the end you who are causing the pain must be the one to tell him it will stop, and then he will answer, or in a very few cases they will not answer, not our fault, no one wants chaos, no one wants the final destruction which carries away everything, including the destroyer, we seek a measured breakdown, a cleansing, like the beams of light of the car shining now through the night, picking out one by one the drops of rain swept gently away by the windshield wipers, nothing is less violent than torture, nothing more orderly, detached, meticulous, because torture is a function of duty, it verges on boredom, but sometimes necessary boredom, like the slow rotation of a planet, necessary for the order of life to continue, you understand, and that is what we tried, my God, we tried, and worked so hard at trying, and cleaned Algeria out in the end, because by 1958 Algiers was calm again, and we could have kept the flow, quiet and strong, but politics taint people, politicians bend to tiny senses of greed, and they gave up for us, desisted in our name, and we left, and I kept trying to make use of the craft of putting things in order, the need to clear space, rearrange, put back, and so in the end we became teachers, but not only teachers, orchestrators, the hand of God upon the waters, because when you grow, when you age, that is what you are left with, and we were left with taking our sense of order elsewhere, trying out the systems somewhere else, explorers down the Orinoco, Livingstone in Africa, Hatteras at the North Pole, only to say, "I have been there," to give these utopias a place, and then you can find your bearings, as we tried to help Argentina find its bearings, that beautiful lost country adrift at sea, trying, once again, to bring a sense of order into the disorder, but how, how, when those who rebelled were better men than those who stood at the helm, men hiding behind costumes, military costumes, religious costumes, men of tiny intelligence, like Casares, you must remember Casares, smelling of cheap cologne, hair lacquered back like a beetle's elytra, Casares waging war against the insurrection, Casares defending "the ancestral values of the nation", Casares proud of having someone teach him "how to deal with this scum", saying, "We have the heart, you give us the science," saying, "We'll bugger this land into submission," and all the while holding glasses of wine in his country house, the smell of charcoal-burnt meat mingling with the eucalyptus, talking as we walked alone away from the party, past the house and the bougainvillea sprouting like a goitre on the pink wall, down the duck pond abandoned by the ducks, covered in a velvet sheet of green slime, cracked Spanish tiles lining its border, cast-iron frogs meant to spout water, rusted long ago, and down to the edge of his estate, a blue and white tower leading nowhere, and Casares pointed at it proudly and opened a small door, and showed me a tiny dark room where once garden furniture must have been kept, and "Here," he said, "here I did my bit for my country," and I asked what, and he said, "Here we brought them, the students," he had ordered that a group of students arrested in town were to be brought to his own house and interrogated, nothing to know, of course, his men had trapped a random lot, and they had had a feast here, beating and raping and terrifying with no method, no purpose, congenital idiots playing with kittens, and they had almost been found out, Casares said, his wife had heard screams and come out into the garden, "Poor fool," he said, "in her nightshirt, barefoot," and he had sent her back never trying to tell her, to explain, because he never understood what he was doing, and Casares in charge, I realized, would make us fail, would break the order to come, if it ever came, overcooking his meat, overdoing his surveillance, ordering the bodies to be driven off in a truck at night, pursued by the neighbours' dogs, witnessed by frightened recruits, thrown on garbage dumps for gulls to discover, no method, no responsibility, no aspirations, no thought, but we knew we had to persevere, we had to try, teach the likes of Casares to think, to act with a course in mind, and yet we knew from the start there was but little hope, we were working hand in hand with the waste of humankind, like Christopher Columbus, who was given the worst criminals to sail off to the New World with, and who in turn razed that New World to the ground, feeding children to dogs, quartering the Inca king, raping the women, flaying the past, prying open the sick minds of those who seek salvation outside order, all mangled in the end, having like outcasts to escape to foreign countries, to settle in this purgatory, this retirement park of the north, to read and listen to music, pay social calls, watch the sea, and now, once again, found out like an emperor in hiding, to have to seek another refuge, another Arcadia, I know not where, and I tried, I tried, but I could never manage to explain it to your mother, what I felt, my nausea, my reluctance, all meaningless on the larger map of the universe, so full of stars, my feebleness, like Livingstone's malaria or Scott's gangrene, parts of myself fed to the three-headed dog that guards the entrance to the world I quietly long for, a world dark and silent as Proust's emptied dining-room on a hot summer's morning, intimate and all embracing, nestled in the cup of God's hand, where loss will not matter and anguish will be accounted for and time will hold no dominion, and sleep becomes possible, and therefore, my question to you, my Ana, is, knowing all this, becoming who you are, and understanding who I am and what I want, will you, my daughter, come with me?

When the voice ceased, the darkness and silence burst in with such force that Ana cowered. This was the bottom of the sea. She was among the drowned. Phosphorous faces watched her from the dashboard.

"Answer me," said the voice.

And Ana, held back by the seatbelt, said, "No."

Antoine Berence stopped the car by the side of the road. He reached across Ana and opened the door. He undid her seatbelt carefully, letting it slide back into its catch. He bent down to kiss her. He watched her wrap her windbreaker around herself and step out into the night. He reached over again to close the door. Then, with a soft whir as the wheels spun in the mud, the car drove off westwards in the dark.

Ana had no idea where she was. She felt cold, and wet. She looked ahead, towards the disappearing tail-lights, and started walking away in the invisible rain.

ABOUT THE AUTHOR

ALBERTO MANGUEL is an award-winning writer, translator and editor whose publications include *The Dictionary of Imaginary Places*, *The Oxford Book of Canadian Ghost Stories*, *The Oxford Book of Mystery Stories*, *Black Water*, *Black Water 2*, *Dark Arrows*, *Evening Games*, and *Other Fires*. He is a frequent contributor to periodicals in the U.S., Canada, and abroad, reviewing fiction and theater for both print and broadcast media. Born in Argentina Manguel spent the first seven years of his life in Israel. He was educated in Buenos Aires and has held a wide variety of posts as editor and translator in Spain, England, France, Italy and Tahiti. In 1982, Manguel emigrated to Canada. He is now a Canadian citizen and lives in Toronto with his family.